# COMING
# UP
# SH●RT

# COMING UP SHORT

### Laurie Morrison

AMULET BOOKS • NEW YORK

Library of Congress Cataloging-in-Publication Data
Names: Morrison, Laurie, author.
Title: Coming up short / Laurie Morrison.
Description: New York : Amulet Books, 2022. | Audience: Ages 10 to 14. | Summary: Seventh-grader Bea is the star short stop on her softball team, which is going to the league championship, but her world has just been turned upside down by the news that her father has been suspended from his law practice because he used some of his clients' money to pay bills; worse the news has been spread by another lawyer online, and that lawyer happens to be the father of Bea's almost boyfriend, Xander; now her fielding skills are slipping, and Bea does not know which is more difficult—dealing with either pity or snickering from her schoolmates, learning to throw again, or forgiving her father.
Identifiers: LCCN 2021037663 | ISBN 9781419755583 (hardcover) | ISBN 9781647003678 (ebook)
Subjects: LCSH: Softball—Juvenile fiction. | Embezzlement—Juvenile fiction. | Fathers and daughters—Juvenile fiction. | Families—Juvenile fiction. | Friendship—Juvenile fiction. | Forgiveness—Juvenile fiction. | CYAC: Softball—Fiction. | Stealing—Fiction. | Fathers and daughters—Fiction. | Family problems—Fiction. | Friendship—Fiction. | BISAC: JUVENILE FICTION / Family / Parents | JUVENILE FICTION / Social Themes / Emotions & Feelings
Classification: LCC PZ7.1.M673 Co 2022 | DDC 813.6 [Fic]—dc23
LC record available at https://lccn.loc.gov/2021037663

Text © 2022 Laurie Morrison
Baseball image courtesy Antonov Maxim/Shutterstock.com
Page ii–iii and back jacket flap: image courtesy NTL studio/Shutterstock.com
Page vi: image courtesy natsa/Shutterstock.com
Book design by Deena Fleming and Chelsea Hunter

Printed and bound in U.S.A.
10 9 8 7 6 5 4 3 2 1

Amulet Books® is a registered
trademark of Harry N. Abrams, Inc.

**ABRAMS** The Art of Books
195 Broadway, New York, NY 10007
abramsbooks.com

*For my team: Mike, Cora, and Sam.*

*And for Myles and Clint, my first (and forever) teammates.*

# CHAPTER 1

I pound my fist into the worn pocket of my glove and crouch into fielding position.

This—right now—is what I live for. It's the softball league semifinals, and we're up 5–4 with one out in the last inning. The other team's center fielder just slapped a perfect bunt down the third base line, so she's the tying run, standing on first base and ready to take off. But there's no way she's crossing home plate. There's no way we're giving up this lead.

"One down, Falcons!" I shout. "Play's to first or second!"

The *cack-cack* cheer starts up on our bench and spreads through the bleachers. *Cack! Cack! Cack!* Faster and faster, louder and louder, with more and more people joining in.

That's the sound actual falcons make when they're protecting their nests, so it's a Butler Middle School thing, to yell *Cack! Cack!* when our teams are protecting a lead. I've never heard the chant get anywhere near this loud at a softball game, though, and I freaking *love* it.

Adrenaline courses through my body. All these people are watching us. Parents. Teachers. The whole baseball team. Even Tyson Carter, who hates me because I got him in trouble for not doing any work on our science project, and his friends who groan when I talk too much in class. They're all here, cheering for my teammates and me.

I glance at Emilia, who's playing second base, and wiggle two fingers in the air. She nods and flashes two fingers back.

A double play ends the game right here. If there's any way Emilia and I can turn two, we will.

"Let's go, Falcons!" Coach Yang yells. "Stay focused now. Play smart!"

The other team's batter gets into her stance, bending her knees and wiggling the bat over her back shoulder.

*Right here*, I will her. *Hit the ball to me.*

There are two kinds of fielders—that's what Dad says. The ones who want to make the play with the game on the line, and the ones who hope the ball goes somewhere else because they're scared of messing up.

I never play scared. I always want to make the play.

Our pitcher, Monique, whips the ball over the inside

corner of the plate, jamming the batter. The ball pops off the skinny part of the bat and bounces past Monique's outstretched glove, toward me.

*Yes.*

I charge.

"First! First!" Coach yells.

That's the safe play: tossing the ball to first base to get one out. But the other team's best hitter is in the on-deck circle, up next, and Emilia's ready at second base. I pull my arm back and throw as hard as I can.

*Smack.*

The ball hits the webbing of Emilia's glove and beats the lead runner by a full step. Emilia pivots and launches the ball to first base, just in time.

"*Out! Out!*" the umpire shouts, pointing to second base and then to first, and I leap into the air and scream my lungs out.

"*Yes!*"

Emilia runs over to do our double play handshake, bumping shoulders and then hips and slapping our gloves together.

"You've got *guts*, Bea," she yells over all the noise. "I can't believe you threw to second on a dribbler!"

"It wasn't a *dribbler*," I protest, even though it kind of was.

Emilia whacks my arm with the outside of her glove. "It was definitely a dribbler. Not that I'm complaining!"

Behind home plate, Coach Yang is talking to the umpire.

*Try to turn two if the ball is hit hard, go straight to first if it's not.* That's her rule, and I broke it.

But Dad's the one whose voice I hear in my head when I play softball. And *Dad's* rule is to trust your gut and never second-guess yourself. That's when errors happen, when you let doubt in. I believed I could make that throw, and I did.

My best friend, Jessi, sprints in from center field. "That was *clutch,* Beasy!" she yells. "We're going to the finals!"

On the sideline, everyone is chanting, "Falcons! Falcons!"

Xander Berg-Thomas is there in the front. I spotted him during warm-ups because I basically have Xander Radar, so I *always* spot him. I didn't let myself look back at him the whole game so I wouldn't lose my focus, but I look now, and my already-full heart swells.

The rest of our teammates pile on top of Emilia, Jessi, and me. I end up at the bottom of a mass of sweaty softball players and somebody spikes my toes, but I don't even care. There's nowhere else I'd rather be.

"Great game, Falcons!" Coach Yang calls. "Let's line up and show our opponents some respect."

The other team's waiting, tears streaming down their faces because their season is over. We head over to tell them all good game, and then I scan the crowd for my parents, but I don't see them.

They were here in the bottom of the fifth inning. I saw them cheering after I scored a run. But now, I see everybody else's families except mine, which makes zero sense. My parents wouldn't miss this for the world. *Literally.*

There's a hand on my shoulder—Coach Yang, leading me away from the rest of my team. "That was a risky play, Bea."

And, okay. There. I see Mom's reddish-brown hair and big sunglasses and Dad's red Falcons hat, white shirt, and softball tie. They're standing way far away, closer to the other team's fans than ours. They've folded up their chairs and packed up all their stuff as if they're in a hurry to take off, which is bizarre, but they're here, waving at me. Dad pulls on his earlobe three times.

One. Two. Three.

*I. Love. You.*

I do it back fast and then focus on Coach.

"I need you to play smart," she's telling me.

I nod, but I'm not going to say sorry. That's a Mom thing: not saying you're sorry when you haven't done anything wrong. Mom says apologies should be reserved for "expressing remorse when you've done something you regret," but girls are conditioned to apologize whenever anyone else is the tiniest bit unhappy and it strips away our power, apologizing so much.

"I know the safe play was throwing to first," I say. "But I didn't want to give their best hitter a chance to beat us."

Coach Yang shakes her head. "If *one* thing had gone wrong, though. If your throw had been a few inches off, or if Emilia hadn't been ready for the ball, we would have given away an out. That could have cost us the game."

I take a breath before I speak so I won't sound like I'm talking back. "I did check that Emilia was ready. I wouldn't have thrown to second if she wasn't."

Coach sighs and finally cracks a smile. "It was an impressive play, Bea. Most high school varsity shortstops can't make a throw like that, and you're in seventh grade."

I grin back. "Thanks, Coach." I'm practically bursting with pride as I follow her back to the bench, where she congratulates the whole team.

"We've got a championship game in two short days," she tells us. "But we'll talk more about that at practice tomorrow. For now, get your stuff and grab your people. Let's head to Luigi's!"

We all erupt in cheers, because Luigi's is where we go to celebrate our biggest wins. We sit together at the long tables in front and recap the best moments of the game while we stuff our faces with extra-cheese pizza. And Coach names a player of the day, who gets the game ball as a souvenir and a Nutella-filled dessert calzone.

Everybody heads off to find their families, and Jessi adjusts the clips that hold back the front pieces of her long black hair. "You think I can get a ride with you? My parents are probably going to want to take the goofballs home."

She points to the sideline, where her five-year-old brothers, Jack and Justin, are picking dandelions and shrieking as they rub the yellow part on each other's cheeks.

"Of course. Meet you in the parking lot?"

"Yep!" She bounds over to her parents, and I swap my spikes for sandals, sling my softball bag over my shoulder, and start walking over to the spot where I last saw Mom and Dad.

But when I pass the bleachers, Xander jogs over to me. My skin heats up, my pulse skyrockets, and my stomach goes wobbly—because that's what happens whenever Xander Berg-Thomas is nearby.

It's been like this since March. One day after spring break, he was wearing a new yellow shirt, and Tyson kept calling him "Sunshine" and singing that "You are my sunshine" song. When I looked over, Xander made his eyes wide and shrugged at me, like, "Tyson's the worst, but what can you do?" and *bam*. Wobbly stomach. Too-fast heart. Giant crush on Xander. Maybe it had always been there under the surface, waiting to activate. I have no clue. Jessi's had a bunch of crushes already, but this is new for me and it's *weird*.

Xander's a little out of breath when he catches up to me. "Bea! Hey, great game! You made some sick plays. You've got a cannon for an arm." He reaches out as if he's going to touch my right bicep, but his fingers freeze before they make contact and he blinks at his hand, as if it moved without his permission. His freckly white cheeks turn so pink they clash with his red Falcons T-shirt, and he stuffs his fists into his shorts pockets.

He's nervous. I make Xander nervous.

Jessi keeps saying he's into me, and I think she might be right.

"Thanks for coming," I say.

He shrugs. "I wanted to. I wanted to see you play."

*You.*

He could mean "all of you." As in, the whole softball team. But now his cheeks are even pinker, so I don't think he does. He's standing so close that I can hear his breath go in and out, in and out. I can see the gold glints in his brown eyes and the one tiny tuft of dark brown hair at the back that always stands straight up instead of cooperating with his part.

I love that uncooperative tuft of hair. I want to reach up and touch it.

Somebody calls Xander's name, and when I look over to see who it is, I notice: Dad's car is gone. It was right there in the front of the parking lot, and now it's not.

Dad would never leave a softball game without me, especially not a game as big as this, but the car is definitely gone. He's been super stressed about work, but he always, always says I'm more important than any client. I can't think of any reason why he'd just *go*.

"One minute!" Xander calls to his friends, and then he turns back to me. "I saw you at the batting cages last weekend, with your dad. I don't think you saw me. You were in the zone. But I think you love softball as much as I love baseball. I like that." He winces. "That came out so dorky. I don't even know why I said that."

Past Xander's left shoulder, Mom's pacing. Two steps one way, turn, two steps the other.

I split into two Beas. One Bea is thinking Xander is really, really cute when he's nervous, and I *did* see him at the batting cages last weekend, because hello: Xander Radar. And I like that he loves baseball so much, too, and I like *him*. A lot.

But the other Bea needs to know where Dad is and why Mom is pacing and what the heck is going on.

Worried Bea wins.

"It didn't sound dorky. I actually . . . I wish I could keep talking to you. Seriously. But I have to go."

"Oh!" he says. "Um, okay?"

I take off toward Mom, who stops pacing when I get close.

"Bea! What a game, honey!"

Her smile spreads wide. Anybody who doesn't know her would think she's fine, but this isn't her real smile. It's the fake one she glues on when somebody says something rude about an article she's written or when people comment about how different she is from Dad's first wife, who grew up here in Butler and died a long time ago. Mom's fake smile stretches wider than the actual one, but it doesn't crinkle the corners of her eyes.

She pulls me in for a hug, and I can feel her heartbeat, hard and fast.

"Dad had to head home, and we need to go, too. I'll get us a ride, okay?" She punches at the car share app on her phone. "A car should be here in a few minutes."

*A car?*

She says this as if it's a normal thing, but we've only ever used that app to get a ride to the airport or to go from a museum to a restaurant or something when we take a day trip into Manhattan. There is nothing normal about somebody else's car taking us to our own house.

"What about Luigi's?" I ask. "Everybody's going. I told Jessi we'd give her a ride."

Mom sighs and smooths the top of my hair. "I wish we could go to Luigi's. You deserve to celebrate with your team, but . . . something's come up. We need to get home now. Somebody else will give Jessi a ride."

She loops her arm through my elbow, and we take off toward the parking lot. I don't have my softball bag positioned right, so the knob of my bat smacks my tailbone with every step, but Mom is walking so fast I don't have time to adjust it.

"Bye, Bea! See you at Luigi's!" somebody calls.

I pretend I don't hear because what am I going to say? *I can't come because my dad left for some mysterious and urgent reason, and now Mom and I have to go, too, but I have no clue why?*

Maybe Gran needed Dad for something. That's all I can think of. Except why wouldn't Mom tell me that?

"Here we go." Mom points at a gray sedan that's pulling into the lot.

She greets the driver and opens the back door, motioning for me to climb in. We end up all jammed together with my softball bag on my lap and my school bag between us. As the car pulls away from the field, Mom pushes her sunglasses up on her head to look me straight in the eye.

"Dad will explain what's going on as soon as we get home. Everything will be okay. I promise." She reaches over my stuff to squeeze my hand. "We're the better-than-a-dream team. Right?"

That's what Mom and Dad call us: the better-than-a-dream team. They say the three of us are the family they didn't even dare to *dream* of, back when their worlds fell apart.

"Right," I echo.

The driver wants to know whether he should take this turn or the next one, and Mom pushes her sunglasses back down and tells him this one's fine. I stare out the window as we go through the center of town, past Dad's law office, past Gramps's old dental office, and past the tiny park in the middle of the town square with four benches facing each other. "The Bartlett Benches," they're called, in honor of Dad's grandpa—my great-grandfather, Benjamin Bartlett, who served nine terms in Congress and always had time to sit down on a bench for a coffee and a chat with any of his constituents whenever he was in town. If we turned right and crossed under the train tracks, we'd get to Luigi's, but we keep going straight instead.

I take my phone out to text Jessi and see her message from eight minutes ago. *Beasy! I can't find the car. Where are you?*

A new text comes in now, from Xander. *Are u OK?*

And then a new text from Jessi pops up, too.

*OMG Bea. I'm so sorry. Emilia's mom is taking me to Luigi's so don't worry about that. We'll miss you and we love you no matter what!!*

Then there's a whole line of hearts. I read the words a second time and blink at the screen. *No matter what.*

*What?*

"Bea." Mom's voice is urgent. "Put your phone away, please."

"I . . . why? What's going on?"

She squeezes my hand again. "Dad and I will explain as soon as we get inside."

The car pulls onto our street and then into our driveway. Mom thanks the driver and nudges me to open my door.

I grab my things and stumble out, and Mom puts her arm around my shoulders and guides me up our front steps.

For the first time in my entire life, I'm terrified to walk inside my own house.

CHAPTER

2

Dad is sitting in the living room with the lights off.

We never hang out in the living room unless Gran's over, but that's where Dad is. It's like he made it inside and couldn't go any farther.

He's holding his red Falcons softball hat in his lap, curling the brim in his hand. He pops up when he sees us and walks over to hug Mom and then me, long and tight. My heart is pounding so hard I swear it might burst right through my ribs.

Mom flips on the light switch, and I set my bags down right on the floor instead of putting them in the mud room where I'm supposed to.

"Nobody said anything to me," Mom tells Dad. "Or to Bea, either, I don't think. She took out her phone, but only for a second."

Dad closes his eyes while he takes in a long breath. A psych-up breath—the kind I always take before I step up to the plate.

"Bea." He puts his hands on my shoulders, then takes them off and shakes his head. "I can't believe this is happening."

My stomach twists and my throat squeezes and this room is so freaking hot. "*What's* happening?" I ask. "What's going on?"

Dad walks me over to the small, stiff couch across the living room. It's an antique that Gran gave us when she moved out of her house and into her apartment—dainty and uncomfortable. Mom never would have chosen it, because Mom likes things to be functional instead of decorative, but she says it's our gift to Gran to accept Gran's gift to us. She perches on the chair next to the couch, which is just as stiff and dainty.

"We love you more than anything," Dad tells me. "You're our greatest source of happiness. I want all the best things in the world for you. I never want to cause you pain."

I nod because I know all that. My parents met back when they were teenagers and Dad spent a summer on Gray Island—the island off the coast of Massachusetts where Mom grew up. They were friends, but they didn't stay in touch, and eventually they married other people.

But then Dad's first wife died in a car accident and Mom's first husband died of cancer, and everything was tragic and terrible until they found each other again, fell in love, and had me. They even named me "Beatrix," which literally means "she who brings joy."

I've always known how much joy I bring them. I've always known they'd do anything for me.

"I made . . . an error," Dad says. "A few errors. Big ones."

His words come out all choked and shaky. Mom moves over and kneels on the ground next to him because there isn't any room for her on this tiny, fancy couch.

"An error?" I repeat.

An error is what happens in softball when someone drops the ball or makes a wild throw. Errors are part of the game. You have to shake them off and move on. That's what Dad always says.

"Henry. I'm going to explain it to her, all right?" Mom says. "It isn't fair to prolong this."

Dad nods, and Mom tells me how things have been challenging over the past year and a half, since Dad's old law firm was acquired by a bigger one that didn't have room for him, and he started his own practice instead of trying to find a job at another firm. She says his clients haven't always paid their bills when they're due, so there have been stretches of time without much income.

I gulp, remembering how Gran asked if opening his own practice was a wise financial decision.

"Everybody knows you. Everybody loves you," Gran had said when Dad first explained his plan. "You aren't short on friends, that's for sure. But do you really have enough reliable clients who will follow you away from the firm and pay their bills on time?"

"Plus, there are a lot of administrative tasks to stay on top of," Mom goes on. "Things Dad didn't have experience dealing with."

"But that's why you have April's mom, right?" I ask Dad.

My teammate April's mom got laid off from her administrative assistant job at Dad's old firm, too, and Dad brought her on to work for him at the new office.

"For some things, yes," Mom says slowly. "But there are other tasks that only the lawyer can do, and . . ."

She trails off, and Dad clears his throat.

"I was supposed to set up a client trust account," he says. "That's a requirement, to have a special account that's separate from the regular business operating one where you hold on to money that belongs to clients before it gets paid out. And I didn't."

That sounds bad, I guess, if it's an important rule to have an account like that and he forgot or didn't get around to making it or whatever.

But it doesn't sound *terrible*. He could go ahead and make one now.

Except . . . then he says there was a real estate deal recently, and he was supposed to hold on to a whole bunch of money after the client signed a contract but before the deal was final.

"I put the money into my general business operating account," he says. "And then expenses came up—my assistant's salary. Rent for the office. And other clients hadn't paid me, so the account balance was too low." He looks down at his hands, which are shaking so hard the whole couch is vibrating. "I spent some of the money I should have been keeping safe for the deal. Some of the money that wasn't mine."

I gasp. "You stole it?"

He winces. "Not exactly. Not intentionally."

He looks up at the photos on the wall across from us. The "Wall of Bea," Jessi calls it. My T-ball photo from kindergarten. Seven-year-old me at the pool wearing a watermelon-print tankini, my chin-length hair much lighter than it is now and my blue eyes scrunched up from looking into the sun. Gap-toothed, nine-year-old me holding a giant pumpkin. Me wearing my summer softball uniform the summer after fifth grade.

All those happy younger Beas smile down at me as I try to process the words Dad just said.

He spent money that belonged to someone else.

That's pretty much the definition of stealing. Isn't it?

"I didn't realize how little money was in the operating account. The funds were all mixed together. I never meant to use money that wasn't mine."

His voice gets louder and louder as he says this, but then he closes his eyes and runs his hands over his hair, which is in-between hair, just like mine. In between brown and blond, in between curly and straight.

"It was careless," he says, much softer now. "I was irresponsible. The deal closed faster than I expected, and I had to scramble to come up with the money. I delayed the deal."

Now his hands are shaking even harder—so hard that Mom reaches up and holds both of them between hers to make them stop.

"Dad came clean right away," she says. "With everyone. We sold off some assets to get the funds we needed. We gave the money back as quickly as we could. Dad's cooperated every step of the way."

My throat is dry and tight, and I can't breathe in enough air.

Every step of the way? How many steps have there been? How long has this been going on?

"I've been working through an agreement with the Disciplinary Review Board, and we finalized things this week," Dad says. "My license to practice law is suspended for a year."

Suspended. Dad's *suspended* from being a lawyer, like a kid who's done something bad at school.

"We were planning to tell you this weekend," Mom says. "But news spread fast."

I glance back and forth between them. "What does that mean? When did news spread? How?"

Dad examines his shaky hands, sandwiched between Mom's, instead of looking at me.

Mom lets go of his hands, stands up, and perches back on the edge of the pretty old chair. I watch her close her eyes and breathe. *I can be calm and in control, I can be calm and in control.* That's what she tells herself when she needs to regulate her emotions so her words come out right.

"There was something on social media," she says finally. "Whoever runs the school's Instagram account posted a picture of Dad at the game, cheering on your team. The other lawyer who was involved in the deal replied, not very kindly."

I blink. Another lawyer told everyone on *Instagram* what Dad did? On my *school's* post?

My phone is zipped inside the outer pocket of my backpack, which is slouched against the wall across the room. I need to see this for myself. I need to know what everyone else already knows.

"I'm sorry, Bea," Dad says. "If there were any way I could go back and do things differently, I would."

*A do-over.*

That's the phrase that pops into my head. When I was younger, Sunday afternoons were Dad-and-Bea times. We'd get out our gloves and have a catch, no matter how hot or cold or rainy it was, and then we'd usually play cards, just like Dad did with his grandpa when he was a little kid.

Whenever he was teaching me a new game, we'd play with our cards faceup on the table, not hidden in our hands, and if I made a mistake, he'd say, "You know, Bumble Bea, I see an even better choice you could make. How about a do-over?"

*Dad* needs a do-over now. He needs to go back and set up the account he was supposed to make. Sell off whatever "assets" he and Mom had to sell *before* his business account was out of money, not after. Or maybe do what Gran said in the first place and look for a job at a different firm instead of hoping he'd be fine on his own.

He needs a do-over, but that's not the way things work in the real world. You can't rewind and change what you did—not on the softball field if you bobble the ball, and definitely, *definitely* not with something like this.

"People make mistakes," Mom says. "This mistake doesn't define Dad, and it certainly doesn't define our family. No matter what anyone says."

But this mistake feels so far from everything that *does* define Dad. Dad has visited Gran every week since Gramps died two years ago so she won't be lonely, even though she spends most of his visits complaining and criticizing. He comes to all my softball games and scrimmages even when he's busy. He runs the Parents' Association at my school. He's a leader and he's a helper and he's *good*. But this thing he's done seems really, really *bad*.

Except he didn't *intentionally* take the money. And other people didn't pay him when they were supposed to, so that's their fault, too.

Mom's phone rings.

"It's Lynn," she says. "My friend who does public relations. She's going to help us figure out how to manage the situation. How to put together some kind of statement. Control the message in whatever way we can."

She goes into the kitchen to answer, leaving Dad and me alone.

He gives me a tight smile. "If anybody can control the message, it's Mom, huh?"

I nod, because Mom is big on controlling *everything*, messages and otherwise. She believes in checklists and structure and self-regulating. If anybody can figure out how to manage this situation, it's probably her.

"Why don't you go shower and change?" Dad suggests. "I'll order dinner. Thai Kitchen delivers, right? You want veggie pad thai?"

I tell him that sounds great even though my stomach is too queasy to eat anything, and then I hug him, grab my backpack, and rush upstairs to my room, where I pull out my phone.

There's another text from Jessi, asking how I'm doing and telling me to call, but I dismiss her message and find the post on Instagram.

It's from the Butler Middle School Athletics Department's account.

There are two pictures: one of me, pumping a fist in the air after I crossed home plate. And then a close-up of Dad, wearing his Falcons softball hat and cheering. The caption says, *7th grader Bea scores the go-ahead run in the 5th inning. Butler Middle alum, Parents' Association Prez, and current Butler parent, Henry Bartlett, cheers for his daughter and her Falcon teammates. #FalconPride #CackCack*

And . . . *no.*

No, no, no, please. No.

The first comment is from Brent Thomas. As in, Xander Berg-Thomas's dad. *He's* the other lawyer.

*The school should check out the NJ Attorney Disciplinary Review Board summaries from this week and rethink whether Henry Bartlett is an appropriate Parents' Association president for a school that boasts about having an HONOR code.*

My heart thuds against my ribs, and my finger wobbles as I scroll down.

Other people commented. Someone asked Xander's dad what he was talking about, and he replied with a quote from the "disciplinary stipulation" Dad reached with the "Office of Attorney Ethics." It's filled with words like "negligence" and "violate" and "suspension."

*Xander's dad* is the reason news spread today.

I met him at school once, and he was *nice* to me. He said he'd heard I was a heck of a softball player and he knew my dad. But Dad messed up so badly that he has a disciplinary stipulation from an ethics office and Xander's dad made sure everyone knew it.

I scan the rest of the comments. An eighth grader who's friends with Emilia wrote, *OMG whut?* and Tyson's friend Liam wrote, *Yikes! LOL.*

*LOL?*

There's a comment from Tina Sugihara—Jessi's mom—saying people should communicate their concerns to the school privately and be respectful of Dad's family. But then my teammate Monique's mom said she's tired of privileged white men thinking rules don't apply to them, and a bunch of other parents said the school should delete this post.

I don't know if they want the school to delete it because they don't want anyone saying bad stuff about Dad or because they don't want anyone to see a happy picture that makes him look like a nice person and a good father. But he *is* a nice person and a good father. He *is*.

I try Mom's trick, closing my eyes and telling myself I can be calm and in control. When that doesn't work, I walk over to my desk and take out the folded piece of paper that's hidden at the bottom of the top drawer.

It's a photocopy of Allison Marie Holcumb's eighth-grade yearbook photo from the 1988 Butler Middle School Record. Last year, I told the school librarian I wanted to see pictures of my dad in middle school. She showed me the shelves with all the old yearbooks, and then when nobody was looking, I snuck over to the copy machine with the one from 1988 and copied Allison's picture.

I look at her poufy bangs, the pearl earrings I imagine she borrowed from her mother, and her friendly smile that shows a mouth full of braces. The smile makes her look like somebody I would be friends with if we were the same age, but the truth is that I'm only here because she's not.

Allison and Dad knew each other when they were kids, and once they were grown-ups, they fell in love and got married and were going to have a baby boy. But then Allison was driving home from work on a snowy day when she was six months pregnant, and a truck driver spun out on black ice and crashed into her car. She died, and the baby died, too, and it was a horrible, devastating tragedy.

And if it hadn't happened, I wouldn't exist.

My parents have framed pictures of Allison and Mom's first husband, Evan, on a shelf in their bedroom. We always have their favorite desserts in their honor on their birthdays: cheesecake on Allison's birthday in October and brownies for Evan's in April. But Mom and Dad get sad and worried if I ask too much about them, so I hold on to this secret photo, just for me.

It always puts things in perspective, looking at Allison's eighth-grade picture. It always reminds me that I need to appreciate how lucky I am because things could be so, so much worse.

I'm here. I have Mom and Dad. I have Jessi and the rest of my team. I have softball and my own room in a nice house and my favorite food that Dad ordered for dinner.

Dad messed up, but he's *Dad*. He loves Mom and me so much. We're the better-than-a-dream team, and we can get through whatever happens now. My parents have already handled the worst things imaginable. They can definitely handle this.

I put the picture back in the drawer, take a shower, and change into clean clothes.

I glance up at the poster on my wall of my favorite softball player, Rose Marvin, looking fierce as always in her U.S. national team uniform. I will myself to be as tough as Rose, and then I head downstairs to eat veggie pad thai and talk about softball. To be Dad's Beatrix and bring him joy now, when he needs it most.

# CHAPTER 3

The next morning, Mom drives me to school. Dad usually takes me before he heads to his office. The morning after a big win, we usually stop at Donut Haven—or "Donut *Heaven*" as Dad calls it because the donuts are that good—to pick up treats for my whole team. But Dad isn't going to the office today. I don't know if he's even gotten out of bed.

In the car, Mom talks too much and too fast. She tells me the school deleted the Instagram post, which is good, I guess, except everyone already saw and the school can't delete people's memories. She says Public Relations Lynn had great advice and they'll finish up a written statement today to post online. She says no one was financially or physically harmed by Dad's mistake, since he gave back the money and the deal still went through. She keeps promising and promising that we'll figure things out, and we'll be fine.

I want her to stop talking, but I don't know how to say that. I wish I were a cute little kid like Jessi's brother Jack, who used to say, "I'm turning off your voice" when he wanted someone to be quiet. Nobody's feelings were hurt—everyone just laughed.

When we pull up to the school, Mom leans over to kiss the top of my head. "My strong, brave girl," she says. "Remember, you can't control what anyone else says or does. But you can always control how you react."

Mom tells me that all the time. Whenever Tyson and his friends are being jerks, or if Gran says something that hurts my feelings, or if I think an umpire made an unfair call or I deserved a better grade than I got on an essay.

"I'll remember," I say, hugging her goodbye.

But as soon as I walk inside the school and turn down the seventh-grade hallway, my Xander Radar goes off. There he is, standing with Monique by the gross water fountain that dribbles out warm water that tastes like rust. They're hunched in close together, whispering.

Monique and Xander are friends. They talk a lot. They could be talking about anything, but I think they're talking about me.

Monique whispers something, and Xander shakes his

head. Then they both spot me. His eyes go wide, and she looks away fast.

They're definitely, definitely talking about me.

I will myself to be strong and brave. I keep my head up high and hold Xander's eye contact.

"Oh! Hi," he says.

That's all.

"Hey, Bea!" Monique's voice is *extremely* cheerful. "We missed you at Luigi's. Coach gave me the dessert calzone, but I bet it would've been yours if you'd been there. I'll buy you one next time we go."

"Thanks," I say. "You deserved it, though. You pitched great."

She shrugs. "You ready for tomorrow's game?"

"Of course," I tell her.

"Yeah, you are!"

She holds up one hand for a high five. After our palms hit, her long brown fingers squeeze my shorter white ones, and I think I feel in that squeeze that Monique is still my friend and my teammate. She couldn't have been saying anything bad, I don't think, even though her mom made that comment on Instagram. She's got my back.

But then the bell rings, and Xander mumbles a "see you later" and bolts, and Monique takes off, too.

The whole rest of the day, I feel everyone's eyes on me.

Nobody says anything mean to my face, but I hear whispers I can't make out when my back is turned. Tyson Carter gives me a weirdly sympathetic wince-smile that makes me want to smack him, and a few people ask if I'm okay. Jessi asks so, *so* many times, and when we're walking out to the field at the end of the day for practice, she says, "I'm so sorry this is happening. This is so messed up."

*This.* That's what she calls it.

Our English teacher, Ms. Markell, circles the word "this" if we use it by itself in our essays. "What is *this*?" she writes in the margin, or "Avoid vague *this*!" She says it's taking the easy way out, just writing "this" and assuming someone else can figure out what you mean.

"You don't have anything to be sorry for," I tell Jessi.

"Okay, well, neither do you," she points out. "Your dad's the one who did something bad."

And that's true, but the words shatter my heart because Jessi *loves* my dad.

He used to take us on surprise adventures when we were younger. We'd get in the car and Dad would start driving somewhere exciting, but we could only ask yes or no questions to figure out where. One time it was the Statue of Liberty. Another time it was the science center, and another time it was a college softball game. I want to remind Jessi about those surprise adventures. I want to tell her she might still be in a batting slump without him, because he's the one who helped her figure out that she was pulling her head up too early instead of watching the ball until it hit her bat.

I don't want her to think anything bad about Dad. I don't want anyone to think anything bad about Dad.

"I'm really glad he doesn't have to go to jail," she whispers, and I stiffen.

*Jail?* There's no way that was a possibility. Is there?

"Maybe he can get another job he'll like more than being a lawyer," she adds. "Like, he'd be a really good softball coach. Don't you think? Or doesn't he always say he wants to write a book about his grandfather and New Jersey politics and stuff? Maybe he can do that."

I stare at her. "The suspension's only for a year. He can go back to being a lawyer when it's done."

Jessi's forehead crinkles, and she unfastens and then refastens one of her hair clips. "Oh."

I don't like the way that "oh" sounds. It's the kind of "oh" that really means, "If you say so" or "That's not what *I* heard."

"What?" I demand.

She holds up both hands, palms out. "My parents were just saying last night that a suspension sort of ends a law career usually. Because it'll kind of . . . you know. Mess up his reputation, and then he won't be able to get clients to hire him."

My mouth falls open, and Jessi bites her lip.

"Maybe they don't really know, though," she says quickly. "Or maybe I misunderstood."

But Jessi doesn't just misunderstand things, and they probably *do* know. Jessi's mom is a lawyer, too. She and Dad used to work together, and now she's a partner at the bigger firm that acquired their old one—the bigger firm had room for *her*, even though they didn't want Dad.

We're almost at the field now. Emilia and Monique are right in front of us. April and Priya are right behind us, and suddenly I think of April's mom.

If Dad doesn't have a job anymore, then April's mom doesn't, either. Mom said in the car that no one else was harmed by Dad's mistake, but April's mom must have been harmed if she lost her job.

My heart is racing and my body feels too hot.

I can't do this right now. I can't think about any of this when it's time for softball practice and we have our biggest game of the season tomorrow.

"I'm sorry," Jessi says, her eyes filling with tears. "I didn't mean to upset you."

"It's fine," I reply, way too loud. "Can we just focus on softball? Let's warm up. Okay?"

Jessi nods and sniffles, and then she jogs off to grab a ball. We start close together, tossing the ball back and forth softly, and then back up once our arms are loose enough to throw from farther apart.

Dad's the person who taught me how to throw a softball. How to hold it in my right hand with the pads of my fingertips on the seams. How to pull my arm back, rotating my torso so I can see the ball behind my back shoulder, and how to bring my hand forward, curling it in close to my ear, as I rotate my torso the other way, step with my left foot, and let go. He's the one who taught Jessi, too.

Dad says you don't have to be big and strong to throw the ball hard or hit it far. The most important thing in softball is your motion. If you use the right form, you build up all the momentum you need, even if you're on the small side like Jessi and me.

I don't break down each step of a throw in my head anymore. But after Jessi and I have been throwing back and forth for a while, I picture Dad sitting in the living room with the lights off yesterday, and I remember those terrible comments on Instagram, and my brain glitches.

The ball feels wrong in my hand. My grip isn't right.

What if I try to throw the ball, but I don't pull my arm back far enough, or I curl my hand in too close to my ear?

What if I over-rotate or under-rotate my torso? What if I let go a split-second too early or too late?

Suddenly, it feels like so many tiny elements have to come together to make one simple throw. I can't believe the risk I took yesterday, going to second base on that dribbler. Coach Yang is right: If one thing had been off, I could have cost us the game.

"Bea?" Jessi calls. "Are you going to throw the ball back?"

"Yeah. Of course!"

I tell myself to throw the freaking ball back to my best friend, but I still just stand here, examining the red seams and the gray-black scuffs on the leather.

"Beasy?"

Jessi's voice is high-pitched and worried. Everyone's looking.

All my muscles tense, and that's a good thing, actually. Anger flashes in my stomach like lightning, hot and bright. I don't know *why* I'm angry, but the feeling dims all the doubts in my head, and I throw, grunting as I let go of the ball.

Jessi gasps when it hits her glove.

"Whoa!" She lets out a nervous laugh.

"Sorry!"

The ball smacked the palm of her glove, not the

webbing, and it must have stung. I *am* sorry if I hurt her hand. But I'm not sorry about the throw. Because it was on target, thank goodness.

That was a weird brain blip, but it's done now. I'm fine.

Coach wants us rested for the championship game tomorrow, so practice is shorter than usual. I text Mom to see if she can come get me early, and she writes back that she's on a call but she'll be here as soon as she can. Our house is only two miles away and it's a nice day, though, so I tell her I'll walk and take off.

My backpack is heavy and my softball bag is, too, but it feels so good to move. The slap of my shoes against the pavement empties my brain, and the afternoon sun warms my skin.

But then a car horn beeps, and it's Dad, pulling up next to me. He rolls down the window. "Hey there! Want a ride?"

There's no way I can tell him I *don't*. So I force a smile, toss my bags in the trunk, and get in.

He leans across the console between the two front seats to hug me. "How are you holding up, Bumble? How was today?"

I blink away the bad parts and tell him, "It was okay."

Dad's in-between-brown-and-blond hair is really in

between the old sandy color and gray these days. His face is pale, and there are purple circles under his eyes. He looks sad and tired and old, and for the first time I can remember, I don't know what to say to him. I want to ask what's happening with April's mom and whether she'll be able to find another job. I want to ask how *he's* doing and how today was for *him*. But I'm scared of how he'll answer any of those questions. I'm scared I'll make him feel worse.

We pass through the center of town. Past the law office he doesn't need anymore and the building where Gramps's dental office used to be. Past those Bartlett Benches in the square.

A couple of months ago, we sat on one of those benches drinking Oreo milkshakes, and Dad told me it's a special thing to live in this town where our family's been for generations and the name "Bartlett" really means something.

"But there's pressure that comes along with everyone knowing us," he said. "Nobody but you gets to decide what it means to be Bea Bartlett. You remember that, all right?"

I thought it was kind of strange when he said it. But he must have been freaking out about money. He must have been worried about letting people down, not living up to his name and what everyone expects of him.

When we're almost back home, his phone rings from where he's stashed it in the cupholder between our seats and I see the name on the screen. Gran. He hits decline and flips the phone over.

"I'll talk to her later. I've talked to her already. Many times today."

I wince. "Is she really upset?"

He sighs. "Yes."

I kind of want to throw Dad's phone out the window so Gran won't be able to reach him.

I know she loves Dad a lot. I've heard her tell people how strong he is to have gone through tragedy and found a way to thrive. I've heard her say he deserves every possible happiness after all that loss.

But I've *also* heard her say that if he hadn't left work early so many days to watch me play softball, maybe there would have been a place for him at his old firm after the merger. And that she'd thought he might be following in his congressman grandfather's footsteps when he became a lawyer, too, but so far *that* hadn't panned out. She's always listing other people's achievements—Uncle Andy's, her friends' children's, Dad's second cousin Jennifer's—as if there's a competition between Dad and every other grown-up she knows, and Dad's never in the lead.

Dad turns onto our street and parks in the driveway, but he doesn't budge from his seat.

"I resigned as Parents' Association President today," he says.

"Oh," I reply.

I'm not sure what to say next. *Okay? Thanks for telling me? I'm sorry to hear that?*

Dad *loved* being Parents' Association President. He was so proud when the school asked him. He had so many big ideas and he recruited so many other parents to get involved. He always picked up coffee and donuts on the mornings when they had meetings at the beginning of the day, and he was so excited to add all the Parents' Association events to our family whiteboard calendar. And now that's over, too.

"Listen," he says. "I want to ask you a question about tomorrow." He's looking at his hands, which are still gripping the steering wheel even though he doesn't need to steer. "You know there's nothing I love more than watching you play softball. But . . . do you want me to be there for the game? Would it be easier if I skipped this one?"

*Oh.*

Before this moment, I didn't think about whether Dad would come to my game tomorrow. He's literally been at every game I've played in, *ever*. But if he shows up tomorrow, will people stare and whisper? Will anyone say something mean to his face?

He sighs. "You shouldn't have to make this decision. Mom's friend Lynn thinks taking a step back from any kind of public event makes sense, until things blow over. She suggested—and Mom thought so, too . . . that maybe it would be better for me to stay home tomorrow. So I won't come. Unless you decide that feels worse to you."

I look out at our backyard, where Dad and I have spent hundreds of hours throwing a softball around. Thousands of hours, maybe.

Softball is part of who I am—it's the thing I'm best at and the thing I love most. But it isn't just *my* thing. It's Dad's *and* my thing. I don't have a single softball memory that he's not part of. But I hate the idea of him sitting in his red folding chair tomorrow, surrounded by people who think he's a thief and a disappointment when he *isn't*. That isn't who he is.

I take a shaky breath. "Okay. I guess it makes sense for you not to come."

Dad lets go of the steering wheel and turns toward me, gripping my hands instead.

"I'm so sorry, Bea. You're the best kid in the world, you know that?" he tells me.

He says that all the time.

"I know you and Mom *think* that," I say back, just like always.

*You think she hung the moon.* That's what Gran some-times tells him, and I finally looked it up. It means think-ing someone is so amazing that they're capable of doing *anything*—like, they might actually be the one who put the moon in the sky.

Whenever Gran says that, Dad says, "For us, she did."

So simple and sure.

We go inside and eat leftover Thai food and play game after game of cards. I don't care that I should be studying for final exams, which start next Monday, because Dad needs *me* to cancel out the comments from people like Gran and Xander's dad and even Jessi's parents.

Dad needs me, and that's the most important thing of all.

# CHAPTER 4

The next day, we're all supposed to change into our softball uniforms at the end of lunch so we can leave for the championship game as soon as our last class is dismissed.

When I come out of the locker room in my red away jersey and white softball pants, I bump right into Xander. I literally bounce off him, stumbling backward.

He reaches out, touching my upper arms for a second before he stuffs his hands in his pockets. The momentary contact sends a jolt down to my fingertips, and I shiver, even though the hallway's warm.

"Hey." He's standing close, looking right at me, and my heart starts hammering. He has a couple of green glints in his brown eyes, in addition to the copper ones. There are more freckles on the bridge of his nose now that the weather's warmer and sunnier, and I'm thinking I like his freckles at least as much as I like the uncooperative tuft of hair, but then I remember what his dad wrote on Instagram. What his dad thinks of my dad. What *he* might think, too.

"Um. Good luck this afternoon," he says. "I hope you win."

An eighth-grade math class gets dismissed from the room across the hall. Kids pour out, loud and happy. Taking up all the space around us, breathing up all the air.

"Oh. Thanks," I say.

He nods. "Also, I'm really sorry about what my dad said. And what your dad did, and how he can't be a lawyer now. And, you know. Everything. I hope you're okay."

He says the words so fast it's hard to understand them. He's talking at least as quickly as he did during his oral presentation in history class last week, when he obviously couldn't wait to finish and sit back down.

Two days ago, he told me he liked how much I love softball. He was about to tell me how much he liked *me*. I'm sure of it. But now he takes off down the hallway before I can say anything. I watch him speed away, his hands stuffed into his pockets and his navy backpack bouncing on his back.

I lean against the cool cinderblock wall and remind myself that there are way worse things in the world than

Xander and me not being . . . whatever we almost were. But there's an empty, aching hole behind my ribs where it feels like he's carved out something I really, really didn't want to lose.

When I get on the softball bus at the end of the day, I claim the row Jessi and I always take—right behind the coaches at the front, because Jessi gets carsick if she sits too far back.

After a couple of minutes, she slides in next to me.

"How's it going?" She almost whispers the question, and she sits at the very edge of the seat, as if she's afraid to get too close to me.

I shrug.

"Is your dad coming today?" she asks, even more quietly.

I shake my head.

"That's probably good, right?" she says. "Or, I mean. Better than if he was there? Like, because it might be distracting or weird or . . ."

She trails off, and every muscle in my body tightens. I want to grab my things, hurdle over her legs, and take off for the back of the bus to get away.

Jessi and I are supposed to be the Power Pair. That's what our parents call us because we're better together than we are apart. We do better on tests when we study with each other. We do better on group projects when we're in the same group. We hit better when one of us comes right after the other in the batting order.

When she had to skip seventh-grade movie night to babysit her little brothers, Jack and Justin, I skipped it, too, and we babysat together. When I messed up the poster I had to make for my science project, she came over with extra poster board and helped me make a new one.

Usually, good things are more fun if Jessi's with me and bad things are easier, but right now, I feel worse with her next to me.

"Maybe it isn't better," she says, her cheeks pink now. "I don't know what to say, Bea. I want to be here for you, but . . ."

She trails off again. "But what?" I snap, and she flinches. "I don't know."

My phone lights up with a good luck text from Dad, just like he always sends on game days.

*Go get 'em today, Bumble! Love you so much!* He even made a graphic, a cute cartoon bee with a softball glove. It must have taken him a while to make . . . but I guess he *has* a while now, with no job and no Parents' Association.

I turn my phone facedown on the seat next to me.

"Look, I just want to think about the game right now, okay?" I tell Jessi. "Not anything else."

Jessi nods, and the bus door closes. Coach Yang calls out, "Here we go, Falcons! Next stop, the championship game!"

Monique gets everybody going with a *cack-cack* chant, and Coach lets Emilia play her psych-up playlist over the bus speakers.

As the bus speeds down the highway, Jessi faces straight ahead and I look out the window, trying to visualize myself on the softball field, making diving catches and turning double plays and crushing the ball at the plate.

I try *not* to picture Dad at home by himself, missing the biggest game of my life. But it's a whole lot easier said than done.

# CHAPTER 5

The championship game is a half hour away, so I wasn't expecting a big crowd from Butler. But since all the other teams' seasons are done and no one else has games, the athletic department used the extra buses to bring any kids who want to watch.

As we're finishing warm-ups, the buses arrive, and an endless stream of people pours out. Lacrosse kids, artsy kids, the whole track team. And the baseball team, too. Including Xander.

My pulse gets fast and my skin heats up, but I pound my fist into my glove, hard, because there's no point in going on Xander alert anymore.

"Wow," Jessi says as we walk over to the bench together.

Emilia bounds up behind us, putting one hand on my shoulder and one on Jessi's so she can launch herself high in the air between us. Her curly ponytail whips around as she jumps, and her hat slips down over her forehead. She laughs as she fixes it.

"Do you see all those people? They're all here to see *us*."

She's so amped up. That's how I felt when I looked over at the packed stands at the semifinals two days ago—like I had springs inside my cleats. I want that adrenaline rush to hit now, but it doesn't. Not when Coach gives us her psych-up speech. Not when the other team takes the field and the game begins.

I imagine the poster on my bedroom wall of my favorite softball player, Rose Marvin, who grew up on Gray Island, just like Mom, and plays shortstop, just like me.

Rose once went 3 for 4 in a game in the College World Series and made an incredible diving catch, and after the game it came out that she had food poisoning and ran into the locker room to puke between innings. If she could play with food poisoning, then I can play without Dad.

The top of the first inning goes too quickly. Emilia leads off, and she swings at a high pitch and pops up to first base. Our second batter strikes out, and our third smashes a line drive to the outfield, but the left fielder's there to make the catch.

That's it. Three quick outs and we're on the field.

I tell myself to play fearless, like always.

I tell myself I want the ball to come to me. I want to make the play. Of course I want to make the play.

"Let's go, Falcons!" I shout. "No outs, play's to first. Here we go, Monique! You've got this."

Monique whips a pitch over the plate and the batter whiffs.

Her next pitch is high, and the batter lays off. The third pitch is hard and low.

*Crack.*

The ball soars up the middle, over Monique's head, a spiraling blur. I'm in the air before I even tell my feet to push off the ground, and *smack*. The ball's in my glove. I caught it.

"Out!" the umpire calls.

"Yeah, Bea!" someone shouts.

My heart slows down a little as I toss the ball back to Monique.

This game is in my DNA, my muscle memory, my *soul*. I just need to stay out of my own way, and I'll be fine.

The next batter singles down the first base line. But then the third batter pops up to Jessi in center field and the fourth batter strikes out.

Emilia and I tap our gloves together and jog to the bench. I peek out at the stands. There's April's mom, who probably doesn't have a job anymore. Monique's mom, who apparently thinks Dad's a privileged jerk. And my mom sitting with all the Sugiharas: both Jessi's parents, both Jessi's brothers, and Mom, alone on the end. She sees me looking and does the *I-love-you* triple earlobe pull Dad and I made up. A softball-sized lump lodges in my throat, but I make myself pull my earlobe back.

I'm hitting second this inning. I press my batting helmet down over my skull, way harder than I need to, and take some warm-up swings.

Jessi walks on five pitches, so she's on first base and I'm up.

Usually, I'd be able to hear Dad's voice cheering for me. Yelling, "Here we go, Bea! Let's go, Bumble!"

Even with all these people here, it's too quiet without Dad. But I settle into my stance—knees bent, bat resting on my back shoulder, eyes on the pitcher—and I tell myself I will give everybody a reason to cheer. It won't be quiet anymore after I hit the ball.

My first swing is too hard. I miss and almost lose my grip on the bat. But that's okay. That's why batters get three strikes. Three chances.

The next pitch comes in. I watch the ball until it hits my bat.

*Crack.*

The ball jumps off the sweet spot, soaring over the shortstop's glove and into the outfield.

Sometimes you get unlucky with that kind of contact. You can try to aim for one side of the field or the other, but you can't control where a line drive goes. But this hit falls perfectly—right in the gap between the left fielder and the center fielder, so neither of them can make a play.

I sprint to first and round the base, heading for second as I watch Jessi circle the bases in front of me.

"Home! Home!" the other team's pitcher is screaming.

Their shortstop catches the relay throw from the center fielder and spins toward home plate. As soon as she lets go, I run to third base, and Jessi slides into home plate under the tag. Safe.

"*Yes!*" I yell.

Jessi stands and pumps her fist, then points at me. I pump my fist and point back to her, grinning because we made that run happen, Jessi and me. For this moment, at least, we're the Power Pair.

My teammates are jumping up and down in front of our bench. Behind them, Jessi's mom is holding Justin and her dad is holding Jack, and all four of them are bouncing and cheering. But Mom has her phone up in front of her face, probably taking a video of this moment Dad is missing.

I scan the crowd of kids from school. A bunch of them have probably never been to a softball game before, but they're all here, and my dad, who's never even missed a *scrimmage*, isn't.

I'm not even paying attention when the pitcher winds up and throws her next pitch.

"Bea!" Mr. Healey, the third base coach, claps to get my attention. "You ready to take off if I give you the sign?"

I need to get my head in the game. Monique gets out on a line drive to second base, but then I score on a ground ball to first.

I go through the motions, jumping up and down and hugging everyone. But my heart feels ripped apart and ragged, like the old softball my neighbor's dog tore to bits.

Dad should be here, celebrating with everybody else. Making friends with people's grandparents and siblings. Taking notes on his phone about things everybody on my team does well so he can give each player a specific compliment after the game is done. But he's not.

Our next batter strikes out, so we don't score any more runs, but we're up 2–0.

The *cack-cack* cheer spreads throughout the stands as we jog back onto the field, but it doesn't psych me up today. The infielders start tossing around a ball like we always do while Monique takes her three warm-up pitches, and I miss the ball April throws me from first base because I'm not paying attention.

This isn't me. I need to focus, but I can't.

Monique finishes warming up, and the first batter of the inning walks to the plate. She's the other team's catcher, and she's a power hitter—Coach Yang said she hit a monster home run in their semifinal game. We all take a couple steps back to be ready.

I tell myself I want this girl to hit the ball to me. I tell myself I want to make the play.

Monique launches her pitch, and the girl hits the ball off the end of the bat, in my direction. I scamper a few steps in and crouch down low, putting my glove all the way down so the ball can't skitter underneath. It takes a medium-high hop off the ground, so I pick up my glove to meet it.

But then I look over to the stands, to the place Dad should be but isn't.

I don't watch the ball all the way into my glove the way he taught me. The ball bounces out of the webbing, hits the dirt, and rolls to my right.

I scramble to grab it and hear Coach Yang yell, "Hold the ball! Hold it!"

But I have a cannon for an arm. This power hitter is strong but not fast, and she's still a few steps away from first. A perfect throw would get her out—it would wipe away my error.

I pull my arm back to throw, and my brain glitches like it did yesterday. *I might miss*, I think. *I shouldn't try.* But I can't stop my motion. The ball flies out of my hand all wrong and sails over April's head.

The batter rounds first base, heading for second.

"Go, go!" the other team's coaches shout.

The batter's almost to second base by the time April picks up the ball, so she jogs it in to Monique on the pitcher's mound. No throw.

Shame grips my throat and twists my stomach. Monique made a great pitch, and I wasted it.

"It's all right, Bea," Emilia calls from second base. "We'll pick you up."

I nod, but I'm wondering what Mom will tell Dad about this play and whether all these kids who've never been to a game before think this is the kind of player I am—someone who can't pick up a simple grounder and throw the ball to first base.

"No outs, play's to first," Emilia yells, because I don't.

We *should* have one out with nobody on base. Instead we have no outs and a runner on second, and it's all because of me.

*Please strike out*, I beg the batter.

I don't want the ball. I don't want to make the play.

The count goes full—three balls, two strikes—and then the batter pops up right between me and Priya, who's playing third base. Either of us could get it, and the other infielders are always supposed to defer to the shortstop, but I don't budge.

Priya glances over at me, waiting, before she finally calls for the ball and makes the catch.

Okay. One out.

I crouch into fielding position and beg my brain to shut up and let my body take over.

The next batter swings, and I know as soon as she connects that the ball's coming to me, hard. It bounces once, then pops into my glove.

It's a perfect double play ball.

If I'd just held on to the ball after my first mistake, there would have been a runner on first base, not second. Emilia, April, and I could have turned two right now and the inning would be over.

*Stop. Make the play you have. Don't mess up again.*

I pull my arm back and freeze.

If I had thrown the ball right away, I could have lobbed it to April. But now that I hesitated, I have to throw it hard.

*Arm back, curl your hand in as you rotate, let go.*

"Throw to first!" someone's yelling. "Throw the ball!"

So I do, but I'm trying to compensate for my last throw going too high, and this time I let go too late. This throw is low, bouncing away from April.

I hear gasps from the crowd. Monique groans.

April sprints after the ball, and the runner who was on second base rounds third and scores. The girl who just hit that grounder and should have been out at first is rounding second. She's getting greedy, going for third base.

"Third, third!" Priya shouts when April gets the ball.

"Hold it!" Coach Yang yells. "Don't throw!"

April always listens to Coach, but she must be desperate. She reaches back and hurls the ball across the diamond, but her throw is too high and Priya can't reach. The runner watches it roll away and runs home, then jumps up and down, celebrating all our mistakes.

*My* mistakes, mostly. April wouldn't have tried to make that throw if I hadn't made so many.

Coach Yang comes out to the mound and motions for all of us infielders to gather around.

"Well, now we've got that out of our systems," she says, trying to make a joke.

Monique glares at the ball in her hand as if she wants to throttle it. She's mad. She's probably mad at me, and she has every right to be.

"Shake it off," Coach tells us.

She says the game's barely underway. We have plenty of time to get those runs back and win.

But Monique's frazzled. She walks the next batter on four pitches.

The other team's number nine batter is up—the last batter in their lineup, and the last batter's usually the weakest. This girl is tiny, probably a sixth grader.

"Come on, Monique," Priya says. "Just throw strikes."

Emilia catches my eye. "Let's turn two if we can," she says, and I make myself nod but my brain is screaming, *No, no. I can't, I can't.*

Monique winds up, and her pitch is a meatball: soft, and right down the middle.

The little batter swings and crushes the ball, way over Jessi's head in center field. Jessi sprints after it and hurls the ball into me, and I spin and throw to home plate, but the girl's already scored. My throw was on target this time, but that doesn't matter at all.

A home run. Their number 9 hitter just crushed a home run, and we're down 4–2.

The other team's fans are on their feet: cheering, screaming, jumping around.

Monique throws her glove on the ground, and there are tears sliding down her face. She's our best pitcher, and this is the championship game, and she's imploding thanks to me.

Coach Yang takes her out of the game and calls Jessi in from center field to take over pitching.

"Come on, Jess," Emilia says. "You've got this."

I try to tell myself what I know Dad would say: that this is a fresh start with nobody on base. That we just need to get one out at a time in the field and go one batter at a time when we're hitting. Unlike other sports, you don't have to race against a clock in a softball game. We won't run out of time. As long as we keep chipping away, we can take the game back.

I try to imagine all the errors I've made this inning as marks on a whiteboard that I can wipe clean. I've made so many accurate throws in my life. Thousands of them. So I messed up two throws in a row. Two is a tiny number compared to all those good ones.

The other team is back to the top of their batting order. Jessi gets their lead-off hitter to pop up to shallow right field, so we have two outs. We only need one more.

But then the next hitter grounds the ball to me.

I charge, pick it up, pull my arm back.

And freeze.

"Come on!" someone shouts.

"Throw it!"

"Throw the ball to first!"

But I can't.

I don't throw the ball. I don't do anything.

The batter runs to first and stands there, completely confused.

Jessi sprints over and snatches the ball back from me. "Bea! What the heck?"

She's mad at me, too, and she *should* be. I'm ruining everything. I'm making us lose.

She strikes out the next batter, so the inning is finally over, but no one cheers or high-fives as we walk off the field.

"Bea. Are you okay?" Coach Yang asks when I get to the bench.

I want to tell her I'm fine. I'll do better. Next inning, I'll play like myself.

But when I think about going back out on that field, my ribs press down on my lungs, squeezing out all the air.

I shake my head.

"Honey," she says, and the word sounds wrong. Coach Yang is not the kind of grown-up who calls kids "honey." "I'm going to move Emilia to shortstop, but I'd like to keep your bat in the lineup. I'll put you in right field just for today, all right?"

Right field, where the weakest fielder goes. Banishing me from the infield.

My teammates are clustered together at the other end of the bench, as far away from me as possible. Emilia whispers something to Jessi, who glances at me with worried eyes, and my throat goes so tight I can't swallow.

"I'm so sorry," I tell Coach, and I really, really am. "I can't. I just—I can't."

I pull the brim of my hat down over my eyes, hurrying past my teammates to pick up my stuff.

I focus on the dirt stain down the side of my white softball pants and the way my spikes sink into the grass as I make my way to Mom, whose lips are pressed together so tightly they've disappeared.

"Oh, Bea," she says.

"Can you please take me home?" My voice comes out weak. Tiny.

I've never heard of a player leaving a championship game unless they're so hurt they have to be carried off the field. It's horrible to abandon my team—I know it is. But I can't stay here another minute.

Mom hesitates. "I don't want you to regret leaving."

"Please," I beg.

She nods, gets up, and puts her arm around me. I tell myself to keep my head down as we walk away from the field, but I look up once, and everyone's watching. Xander.

Tyson. Jessi's little brothers. Everybody else's parents. All the other kids from my school.

"That poor girl," a lady I don't know murmurs, and my heart cracks.

I'm not a gutsy, fearless softball star.

I'm a quitter. I'm a head case.

I'm "that poor girl."

## CHAPTER 6

In the car, Mom doesn't say anything for what feels like a very long time.

Cheers erupt from the field behind us, but trees block our view, so I can't see what happened.

Finally, Mom stops at a red light and says, "What a rotten afternoon."

It's such an epic understatement that I laugh.

"Everybody has bad games, right?" she asks.

I raise my eyebrows. "Not like that."

She sighs. "Oh, Bea. My strong, brave girl."

But I'm not strong or brave. If I were, I wouldn't have begged her to take me home. I wouldn't have self-destructed out there in the first place.

"This is so hard," Mom says. "We'll get through this together. I know we will. But this is all so tough."

*This. This. This.*

What Dad did, how he can't be Parents' Association President and maybe can't even stay a lawyer, how I just made more errors in one inning than I have pretty much all season. I imagine my English teacher, Ms. Markell, drawing a red circle around this whole conversation.

The light turns green and the car behind us honks, so Mom gives a little wave and accelerates.

"At least school's almost over," she says after a while. "Not even a full week left, and then it's summer. You can take a step back from everything. Get yourself together. That's something. Right?"

But I can't step back and get myself together—not really. Because I have to spend the last two weeks of July and the first two weeks of August at a sleepaway softball camp in Virginia with Jessi, Monique, and Emilia. Shame clobbers me in the gut when I think about how expensive the camp was and how Dad hesitated when I asked if I could go.

"This is what it costs for a month?" Dad said when he first looked at the website. "Is this a typo?"

He kept telling me "we'll see" and "Mom and I will talk about it." I should have dropped it and stopped asking, but Monique and Emilia had already requested each other as roommates, and Jessi kept saying it wouldn't be as fun if she had to room with someone random. I didn't want to miss out. I didn't want my teammates to get better at softball without me.

I had no idea Dad's clients weren't paying him on time and he was worried about money, but I *did* know he'd do anything to make me happy. I *did* know he can't stand to tell me no.

I shouldn't have kept pushing him when I could tell he was stressed, but I did, and now I'm stuck going to this too-expensive softball camp when all my teammates are probably furious with me and I just abandoned them at the championship game. When I'm not even sure I can throw a freaking ball anymore.

Jessi texts me after the game to let me know we lost, 7–4. She says a bunch of people are going to Luigi's to celebrate our season, even though we lost the game, and I should come if I want.

But there's no way I can face my teammates, and I don't deserve to go out for postgame pizza when I bailed on the actual game. I tell her I can't, and she texts back a frowny face, but she doesn't try to convince me. She doesn't say she'll skip Luigi's and keep me company instead.

All weekend long, Dad keeps saying all athletes get

stuck in their own head sometimes. He rattles off the names of professional baseball players who suddenly lost the ability to throw the ball to first base, and big-name pitchers who woke up one day and couldn't hit the strike zone. "The yips," it's called. He says it's no different from a hitter getting in a batting slump, and he can help me get rid of the yips the same way he helped Jessi when she was slumping at the plate.

But I've looked up those baseball players. Steve Sax, Chuck Knobloch, Daniel Bard, José Altuve. Some of them got over the yips, but others never did.

I hole up in my room all weekend, grateful I have final exams to study for. I cram my brain full of facts and dates and equations. Jessi and I FaceTime to quiz each other for science, but as soon as we finish, I pretend Mom's calling me for dinner so we won't have time to talk about anything else.

Somehow, I get through all four days of exam week. Tyson asks me to toss him an eraser before the math exam and makes a big show of ducking in case I throw it wildly, but that's Tyson: the literal worst. Other people whisper, but I can mostly tune them out.

On Thursday, the last day of seventh grade, I bolt out the door after our Spanish exam. Jessi catches up and asks if we're on for our usual last-day-of-school lunch.

"I told my parents I wasn't sure," she says, fidgeting with the strap of her backpack. "I can take the bus home, or I can come with you if your dad wants to take us to the deli. Either way."

The last day of school is always a half day, and usually Dad picks Jessi and me up and takes us to the deli for Sloppy Joes—the New Jersey kind, not the messy ground beef kind. The New Jersey ones have turkey or roast beef piled high between three slices of rye bread, each spread with Russian dressing and coleslaw, and Dad, Jessi, and I love them.

The deli is right in the center of town, looking out over the Bartlett Benches. It's always packed at lunch time with people who used to be super excited to ask Dad for random legal advice or chat with him about the Yankees, or my softball season, or local politics. Mom used to joke that she had no idea how Dad got any work done considering how long it took for him to eat lunch anywhere in town since he couldn't resist talking to every single person inside a restaurant.

But the deli owner used to be Dad's client, and Dad's barely left the house over the past week. There's no way we're eating there today.

"I don't think the last-day lunch is happening," I say,

and Jessi lets go of the backpack straps she's been messing with as if she's relieved.

"Okay," she says. "Well, we're doing pastabilities at my house tonight if you want to come. You could sleep over?"

I love pastabilities night at the Sugiharas'. Everybody picks which sauce they want—marinara or pesto or cream—and what kind of veggies and precooked meat to add in, and then Jessi's dad mixes each person's pasta separately. He gets four different skillets going all at once, and it's always loud and messy and fun.

But it wouldn't be fun right now. Not when Jessi's whole family saw me self-destruct at the championships, and not when I keep picturing her parents sitting at that kitchen table I've eaten at so many times, telling her that Dad's ruined his reputation and no one will want to be his client anymore.

I tell her I can't tonight but I'll text later, and then I give her a quick hug and rush out to the pickup line, where I find a spot far away from everyone else to wait for Mom. A black car pulls up to the curb, and a sixth grader yells that she'll be right there but then takes forever saying goodbye to all her friends. There's a Gray Island bumper sticker on the car's back windshield: a black *G.I.* and the outline of a lighthouse next to the letters.

Gray Island, the place Mom grew up but never wants to go back to.

Most people who live in New Jersey just go to the shore if they want a beach trip, but some families go farther—to Cape Cod or Martha's Vineyard or even Gray Island. Jessi's family went to Gray Island one summer to stay with her mom's best friend from law school, and there are a few other kids in my class whose families go every year.

I used to love hearing Dad tell the story of how he and Mom met there when they were teenagers. He got a job as a lifeguard the summer between his freshman and sophomore year in college, and Mom and her best friend, Danielle, were helping organize a town event called the Slow Pitch Social—a big Fourth of July picnic and pickup softball game. Mom was walking around handing out flyers, and she gave Dad one and told him to come. He was into Mom from the first second he saw her, and he was a really good baseball player, so he was sure he'd impress her. But he wasn't used to slow pitches, and he was trying so hard to hit a home run that he struck out in his first at bat. Then he struck out with Mom when he tried to flirt with her, because she already had a boyfriend. The whole summer, Dad kept trying to convince Mom that she might like him as more than a friend, and Mom kept telling him it would never happen.

We never go to Gray Island, though. I used to ask all the time if we could, especially once I found out Rose Marvin is from there, too. Rose is enough younger than Mom that they never met, but I thought maybe we'd run into her when she was home visiting her family or something. I've only been once, for my grandfather's funeral three years ago.

But Rose is running a softball camp there that starts really soon. There was an ad in one of my softball magazines, and Dad joked that I should stay with Aunt Mary and go to Rose Marvin's two-week day camp on Gray Island instead of the month-long sleepaway one since it was a fraction of the cost.

Or I thought he was joking, anyway. Maybe he wasn't.

The sixth grader gets into the car with the Gray Island bumper sticker, and an idea pings inside my brain.

What if I *could* go to Rose Marvin's Gray Island camp instead of the one I'm signed up for?

I picture myself on a softball field far away, fearless and free. Like Heather Ferris, a Division 1 college catcher I read about, who was an all-star until her junior year, when she suddenly couldn't throw the ball back to the pitcher anymore. She thought she was finished with the game, but after college she moved to a new state and tried out for a rec league team on a whim, and she was totally fine. Back to her all-star self. Once she started over somewhere new, the yips were gone.

It's probably way too late to join a camp that's about to start. Mom probably wouldn't let me go. But when I imagine escaping to camp on Gray Island, every muscle in my body relaxes.

# CHAPTER 7

Back at home, Mom pulls out a bag of Sloppy Joes that she picked up at the deli.

In the kitchen, Dad's breakfast dishes are still sitting on the counter, and there's an open container of cream cheese on a crumb-covered cutting board. Mom sighs as she puts the cream cheese into the fridge. Then she slides everything else into the sink, closes her eyes, and takes an extra-long breath—probably willing herself to be calm and in control—before gluing a smile on her face and telling me to go get Dad.

I find him in the extra bedroom that doubles as Mom's office. His usually clean-shaven face is covered in stubble that's a few shades darker than the hair on his head. He's sitting at the desk Mom usually uses, staring at the screen of his laptop, but the screen is dark. The computer might not even be on.

"Dad?" I say, but he doesn't hear me. "*Dad!*" I repeat, and he startles.

"Bumble! Hey, sweetheart."

His fake smile is nowhere near as convincing as Mom's. He congratulates me on officially being an eighth grader and follows me downstairs, where the kitchen table is set with the sandwiches arranged on a pretty serving plate in the middle.

"I talked to Rina," Mom tells Dad. "She said Sunday works."

"Sunday," Dad says. "Wow. All right."

Mom helps herself to a sandwich triangle, then plucks out the toothpick, scrapes off the coleslaw, which she can't stand, and turns to me. "Rina's a realtor."

I gaze out the kitchen window at Mom's vegetable garden and the grassy stretch of yard where Dad and I have catches, and I start to understand. Dad can't be a lawyer now, maybe ever. We need money.

"We're thinking about selling the house," Mom says.

I look away from our yard. "That makes sense," I say, but my voice comes out squeaky.

"It's a great house. The best," Dad adds, as if the house

might be offended. "But selling it would take some pressure off."

"And we wouldn't leave Butler," Mom promises. "There are smaller places on the other side of town that we can look at. We'll make sure you don't have to switch schools for eighth grade."

"Okay," I say again. Just as squeaky.

I'm trying my best to be strong and brave—to do what's right for our family. But . . . all my memories are in this house. Mom and Dad have always said we were meant to live here.

When Mom was pregnant with me, they used to walk by this house and fantasize about buying it, but it wasn't for sale. They were about to put in an offer on a different place, but right before they did, they heard this one was going on the market and jumped on it. A better-than-a-dream house for our better-than-a-dream-team family.

But I can deal with moving, for Dad's sake. I need to.

I force myself to pick up a sandwich triangle and chew.

"Rina thinks we should act fast so we don't miss the prime selling season," Mom says. "The sooner we list the house, the better shape we'll be in. We're aiming for an open house on Sunday."

A bite of sandwich sticks in my throat. "Sunday as in three days from now?"

Dad puts his pale, stubbly face in his hands.

"I'm so sorry, Bumble," he says, and he sounds like he might cry. "I'm so sorry to put you through this."

"It's fine. It'll be okay. I'm okay," I tell him.

Because I need to be okay. I need to be his Beatrix and bring him joy. But the walls of this kitchen are closing in on me, and I'm not sure I can handle being here while other people tour through our house to decide whether they want to live here now that we can't. I'm not sure I can handle Jessi's pity or other people's whispers. All I can think about is Rose Marvin's camp on Gray Island. All I can think about is getting away.

I force down the rest of my sandwich, and as soon as I get back up to my room, I find the camp online and call the number that's listed.

"Can I help you?" a woman's voice asks.

I gulp. "Um, I really hope so."

It's surprisingly simple to change from one camp to another. There's room for a few more players at the Gray Island camp, and when I call the sleepaway one next, I find out they have a long waiting list, so my parents can get back most of their money if I give up my spot.

I print out the registration form for the Gray Island camp and hurry back downstairs to show Mom and Dad.

I tell them about the difference in the cost and about Heather Ferris—how going somewhere else cured her yips.

"And this way I can step back and get myself together after what happened at the championships," I say, echoing what Mom told me in the car. "It's an amazing opportunity, to be coached by my softball idol, right? And Aunt Mary always says she'd love to have me stay with her."

Mom's older sister, Aunt Mary, sends me a birthday card every year, and every year, she writes at the bottom that I'm <u>always</u> welcome to visit. The always is underlined, every single time.

"It might be a good thing," Mom says to Dad.

Dad is quiet for a long time, and I start to worry that this idea has made him feel even worse. But finally, he says, "If this is what you want, Bumble, let's call Aunt Mary and see if we can make it happen."

And that's pretty much that.

Aunt Mary's on board. Mom uses credit card points to book my flights. On Saturday morning—less than two days from now—I'll be on my way to Gray Island. I'll get my escape.

# CHAPTER
# 8

When we pull up in front of the departure area at the airport very early on Saturday morning, Dad hands me a bag with three neon yellow softballs inside. They're the cushiony kind we use when we practice in the school gym on rainy days.

"I read that it helps some people with the yips to throw against a wall by themselves," he says. "There's a handball wall at the park near Aunt Mary's. These should bounce right off. You can go there if you want to get some throws in, since I won't be around to have a catch."

*And* since I haven't agreed to throw with him in days, even though he's been around all the time, because I'm so afraid I won't be able to hit his glove.

I fight off the guilt that twists up my gut, and smile.

"Thanks, Dad," I say. "That's a really good idea."

He gives me a wobbly smile back and hugs me goodbye. "Have a great trip, Bumble. We'll miss you so much."

Mom hugs me next and hands me an envelope full of spending money. She tells me to be patient with Aunt Mary, whatever that means, and reminds me never to swim in the ocean if there isn't a lifeguard on duty.

The car behind us honks and someone who works at the airport tells us to move it along, and then they're in the car again, driving away. And I'm walking into the airport, alone.

A few hours later, I step off the plane into the Gray Island airport. It's tiny: only one terminal with a handful of gates.

Aunt Mary is waiting for me at baggage claim. I've met her exactly three times—once at my grandfather's funeral, plus two other times when she and her ex-girlfriend Linda took weekend trips to New York City and we took the train in to meet them for lunch.

She's eight years older than Mom, and they look almost nothing alike. Mom is tall—three inches taller than Dad—with pale, pinkish skin and reddish-brown hair that reaches her shoulders. Aunt Mary is shorter, with chin-length gray-brown hair and a round, tan face. But she grins when she sees me and I swear, she and Mom smile the exact same way.

"Bea!" She pulls me in for a hug. "I'm so glad you're here. Now let's get your luggage and get out of this dinky old airport. It's a beautiful day!"

I follow her toward the exit, wheeling my suitcase along, and hustle to keep up as we cross the street to reach the parking lot.

The air is fresh and salty and cool for summer. A seagull scampers between empty parking spots, pecking at a piece of sandwich crust.

Aunt Mary pops the trunk of a maroon sedan so I can put my bags inside, and once we're both in the car, she turns on the engine. Music blares out of her speakers—two female voices, crooning in harmony. She turns the dial down a little and rolls down the windows.

"Thanks again for having me," I say. "I know it was last-minute and two weeks is a long time."

"I'm thrilled to have you. Truly." She smiles her Mom smile. "To tell you the truth, I'm glad you'll have two weeks here. I want you to fall in love with Gray Island so you'll come back every year and bring your parents. That's my mission. And two weeks should be enough time to achieve it."

She winks at me, and I let out a surprised laugh.

"Also, while we're having honesty hour, there's one more thing I should say," she adds.

"Oh. Um, okay," I reply, but that sounds a little ominous.

She taps her hands against the steering wheel in time with the beat of her music and says, "I'm a talker, Bea. I feel very strongly that anything we're going through is mentionable, and if something's mentionable it becomes more manageable, to paraphrase my good neighbor Mr. Rogers."

She glances at me, so I nod to show her I'm listening, but I have no clue where she's going with this.

"Sometimes I can be a little pushy, trying to get somebody to talk through something when they aren't ready. I've done it to your mom in the past. I don't want to do that to you."

I roll the window up so the sound of the air rushing into the car won't distract me from whatever comes next.

I know Mom and Aunt Mary were close when they were kids and aren't close anymore, but I don't know *why*. Mom always says she and Mary are family and they love each other, but they have their own lives and those lives don't intersect much and that's that. But what Aunt Mary just said makes it seem like something happened. Like they had a fight, maybe. Or more than one fight.

"You and I don't know each other very well yet," she says. "So I want you to know that you can talk to me about what's going on with your dad or softball or anything you want, any time. But I'll try my best not to push you if you aren't ready. And if I do, you tell me to back off. Deal?"

I lean back against the seat, a little disappointed she doesn't say anything more about her and Mom but relieved, too. She isn't *this*-ing me about Dad like Jessi, making me feel like things are too shameful to say out loud. But I don't have to be on high alert, wondering how much she knows and what she'll bring up when.

"Deal," I say. "Thank you."

She turns left at the next light, and we wind through a neighborhood full of gray houses. When we reach the top of a hill, I can see the ocean in the distance—sparkly gray-blue water with frothy white waves rolling toward sand. I roll the window back down, leaning my head out.

"Ah. You're an ocean girl, huh?" Aunt Mary yells over the noise of the wind.

But I'm pretty sure I don't qualify as an "ocean girl" when the most time I've ever spent at a beach is an occasional long weekend when Dad's brother, Uncle Andy, invites us to visit the beach house his family rents every summer at the Jersey Shore.

We go around another bend, and the homes get bigger and fancier. Some are tall and rectangular with towering windows, some have wraparound porches and look like gingerbread houses. They're giant houses squeezed onto not-so-giant yards.

"Those are summer homes," Aunt Mary tells me, pointing out the cars in the driveways with out-of-state plates. New York. Connecticut. New York again. "Empty in the off-season, mostly. And that's the street we'll turn onto to get to the school where your camp is. It's just a few minutes down that road."

"Is it the same school you teach at?" I ask, and she laughs.

"No. I teach at the public high school. Your camp is at *Gray Island A-caaa-demy.*" She says the name funny—in a fake British accent. But before I can ask why, she changes the subject, asking whether I'd rather go straight back to the house or check out the town first.

"Town sounds good," I say because I want to see everything I can. I want to know this place that used to be Mom's home at least as well as every random person from New Jersey who comes on vacation here.

"Great," Aunt Mary says. "Next question: How do you feel about ice cream?"

I giggle. "I'm definitely pro–ice cream."

"Then it's settled. First stop is ice cream in town."

"Ice cream *now*?" It's only eleven, and I haven't had lunch.

Aunt Mary grins. "I'm pulling out all the stops to make you fall in love with Gray Island."

The road changes over from concrete to cobblestones when we approach the downtown area, and the car *bump-bump-bumps* along. I recognize the whaling museum Dad pointed out when we were here for my grandfather's funeral and a coffee place where we picked up breakfast on our way to the ferry the morning we left. But we were here at the beginning of April, and now it's the middle of June. Then, everything was still and quiet. Now, there are people everywhere. Families with little kids riding by on bikes, grown-ups eating brunch at outdoor tables in front of restaurants, teenagers in a cluster outside a bakery.

Aunt Mary pulls into a tiny parking spot, and I follow her down the brick sidewalk past a girl around my age, who's at a table in front of the bagel place with a man who must be her dad. The girl says something, and her dad laughs, long and loud. I'm watching them instead of where I'm going, and I almost trip over a broken brick.

"Here we are!" Aunt Mary says when we reach the next corner. The sign above the door says *The Creamery*, and the name's familiar, but I can't place it.

It isn't open yet, but Aunt Mary waves to someone inside and then turns the doorknob, leading me in. A bell jangles as the door closes behind us, and a warm, sweet smell greets me.

"Oh my gosh," I say.

Aunt Mary beams. "The waffle cones. They're the best in the world. Award-winning. Right, Dee?"

*Dee.* She's behind the counter refilling ice cream toppings and has curly, light brown hair pinned back from her face and a maroon Creamery T-shirt. And now I know who she is. Danielle. My mom's best friend from growing up. This is Danielle's family's ice cream store.

"Well, technically the waffle *cups* won gold," she says.

Then she notices me, and her mouth drops open. She yanks gloves off her hands, puts a cover on the toppings, and rushes over.

"Bea Bartlett! Oh my gosh. You look even more like your mom now than you did when I saw you last."

"I do?" I ask. I'm used to people back home saying I look like Dad.

"So much!" She holds her arms out and comes in for an embrace, then stops herself. "Sorry. My kid says I need to ask. Can I hug you?"

I nod, and she pulls me in close and hangs on. We only met for a few minutes after the funeral, but I've heard a bunch of stories about her. I used to ask Mom to tell me about when she was growing up, since I knew so much about Dad and Uncle Andy's adventures as kids in Butler. She almost never told me about her family, but sometimes she'd tell me funny things she and Danielle did.

"Should I call you Danielle?" I ask. "Or Ms. . . ." I'm not actually sure I know her last name.

"Oh, Danielle's fine. I'll answer to Dee-Dee even, for you." She steps back and looks at me again. "Gosh, what a great surprise. Is your mom here? Your dad?"

I shake my head. "Just me."

"This time," Aunt Mary cuts in. "Maybe next time we'll get the whole family."

"Well, what can I get you, Bea?" Danielle asks. "Anything you want, on the house."

Aunt Mary wags a finger. "Nuh-uh. No more 'on the house.' Not this summer."

Danielle sighs. "Oh, come on. Let me give Bea a special welcome."

I glance between her and Aunt Mary, trying to understand the conversation they're having with their eyes.

"Creamery ice cream is enough of a welcome, and it's on me," Aunt Mary insists, and Danielle finally gives in.

Aunt Mary asks for peach chiffon in a cup, and I scan the list of flavors on the wall. "I'd like black cherry in a waffle cone, please," I say, and Danielle puts her hand on her heart and then waves it in front of her face.

"Look at me, getting emotional over an ice cream order. It's just—Bea here looking exactly like Chrissy used to, ordering the same thing she always got."

I blink. "Wait . . . what?"

"Sorry. *Christina*," Danielle corrects herself.

But that's not what surprised me. I know people used to call Mom Chrissy. "My mom hates black cherry," I say. "She says it tastes like cough medicine. She always gets butter pecan."

Danielle's eyebrows shoot up. Aunt Mary presses her lips together the same way Mom sometimes does and says, "Huh. Well, tastes change, I suppose."

"Sure." Danielle goes back behind the counter to serve us our ice cream, which seriously might be the best thing I've ever eaten. It's creamy and tangy, and the waffle cone is mostly chewy with just the right amount of crunch.

Aunt Mary and I settle in on stools at the counter, and I snap a quick selfie and send it to my parents so they'll know I'm here and happy. I hesitate a second and then send it to Jessi, too, with a message that says, *Hi from Gray Island! First stop: ice cream. Miss you already!*

Jessi just thinks I'm on a last-minute vacation. She doesn't know about the camp on Gray Island because I don't know how to tell her I'm not doing the sleepaway one, where we're supposed to be roommates. I need to tell her. I *will*. It's just . . . I don't want to let her down again, right after I cost us the championships, and I don't want to cry to her about how I needed to get away and make her pity me even more.

"Hey, is Hannah around today?" Aunt Mary asks Danielle. "She's going to that softball camp at the Academy, right?"

"She's at her dad's, but she'll be back in an hour or so. And she sure is. It's the only thing she talks about. Rose Marvin this, Rose Marvin that."

"Guess who else is going?" Aunt Mary angles her head toward me.

"Get out! Chrissy's kid and my kid playing softball together. I love that! Do you remember Hannah, Bea? Tall, dark hair, lots of attitude?"

I nod. She had glasses and super long hair, and she got mad that Danielle wouldn't let her have a second brownie at the reception after the funeral until everyone had gotten a chance to take one.

"I'll have her stop by this afternoon, once she's back on the island," Danielle says as she finishes refilling the tub of Oreo cookie bits.

When Aunt Mary and I finish our ice cream and head back outside, I get a text back from Jessi.

*YUM! Jealous!! We miss you too!*

And there's a picture of her, Monique, Emilia, and April in bathing suits, grinning with their faces smooshed together. I can tell they're at Monique's pool, and there are other people behind them. Tyson for sure, obnoxiously photobombing, but I can't tell who else.

My breath catches. There's half a torso at the edge of the photo that might be Xander's, and now I'm thinking about Monique's mom's Instagram comment, about privileged white men thinking rules don't apply to them. And how I still don't know if April's mom has found another job.

My throat is tight and my breath is jagged, but I will not do this. I won't get all worked up about what's happening at home right now—who might be talking about me or gossiping about Dad or even flirting with Xander.

"Everything okay?" Aunt Mary asks, and I slide my phone back into my pocket.

"Everything's good," I tell her.

Or it will be, anyway. As long as I don't let my brain spiral out of control again. As long as I can focus on *me* and *here* instead of everyone else and home.

## CHAPTER 9

After our ice cream, we grab bagels for lunch and then drive back to Aunt Mary's house. It's the same style as a lot of the other houses around here: gray and sort of boxy with small windows trimmed in white. It's where Mom and Aunt Mary grew up, and then Aunt Mary moved back in to take care of my grandfather and stayed after he died.

Aunt Mary parks on the street out front, and I'm surprised to see a blue SUV with Connecticut plates in the driveway.

"The renters," she explains. "The cottage looks great. It's booked up all summer, almost. Your parents were so generous to help pay for renovations."

Right.

The house is half Aunt Mary's and half Mom's,

technically, and last fall, Aunt Mary asked Mom and Dad if they would help pay for a construction project to convert the detached garage into a cottage that could be rented out in the summers. Dad always supports anything that might bring Mom and Aunt Mary together, but he definitely hesitated when Mom asked what he thought, and I saw him at the kitchen table one day last winter, shaking his head and muttering to himself as he flipped through the contractors' bills.

I wonder if Aunt Mary feels as guilty about asking my parents for money for renovations as I feel about asking to go to sleepaway camp.

I follow Aunt Mary inside the house, breathing in the faint lemony smell and wondering which of these things were here when Mom was a kid. The faded white-and-blue-striped couch? The dark wood coffee table? The tall bookshelves?

There are a few framed photos sitting on an end table. One of Aunt Mary with her ex, Linda, both laughing. I'm a little surprised she has it on display, since she and Linda aren't together anymore. But I don't linger on that because another picture pulls my attention: a photo of two girls. The bigger one has long pigtail braids, and she's holding a grinning toddler in her lap.

"You and Mom?" I ask, and Aunt Mary nods.

Toddler-Mom has straight bangs across her forehead and tiny baby teeth.

"I've never seen a picture of her this little," I say. The truth is, I've barely seen any pictures of Mom as a kid, period. I know exactly what Allison looked like in eighth grade, but not Mom.

Aunt Mary shows me another photo over on the bookshelf—her and Mom at Mom's high school graduation. Mom's hair is lighter than I've ever seen it, and longer. Her face is a little rounder, too, and I think I look more like *this* Mom than the one I know.

Aunt Mary tells me to help myself to anything in the kitchen, and then she walks me up to the bedroom where I'll be staying. It's set up as a home office with a daybed against the wall, but she says it used to be Mom's room, years ago.

She gives me some time to settle in, so I look around a little, searching for signs of the Mom that used to sleep in here. But the shelves are filled with Aunt Mary's teaching books and thick mystery novels, the dresser drawers are empty, and the only things in the closet look like Aunt Mary's winter clothes.

I call my parents, who can only talk for a few minutes because they're busy cleaning up for the open house tomorrow, and then Aunt Mary offers to take me out for a walk.

"I can show you the closest beach and then take you to the park with the handball court if you want. Your dad said you might want to throw?"

I jump up to change my shoes and put my glove and ball in a bag, and she leads me out the front door. She points out the house at the end of the street where Danielle grew up, and then we turn onto a sandy path that takes us to a small beach with a sign that says, "Residents and Guests Only." The breeze is stronger than it was back on Aunt Mary's street, and tiny, ripply waves lap against the pale, soft sand.

"It's the bay," Aunt Mary explains. "That's why the waves aren't big."

My breath syncs up with the slowly swishing water, and something about the salty wind makes my brain extra clear and alert. "It's so peaceful," I say, and Aunt Mary nods.

"Your mom and I used to prefer the beaches on the other side of the cove, with big waves for surfing. But I appreciate the quiet now."

"Wait. *Mom* liked surfing?"

"She sure did. Why?"

I shrug. "She isn't a beach person." Mom always says she'd choose lakes and mountains over the ocean any time.

"Huh." Aunt Mary looks out at the water. "Well, maybe she got her fill, growing up here."

"Maybe so," I say. But it's hard to imagine anyone could ever get their fill of this.

I take off my sneakers and socks and hold them in my hands so I can feel the cool, soft sand cushioning the soles of my feet and clinging to my toes. We walk for a while, and after we turn around to head back the way we came, we pass two girls—eight or nine, maybe—who are carrying pails and collecting shells near the edge of the water.

"No, that's not a good one," the taller one says. "You have to look for the *special* ones."

"They need Mom and Danielle's insider shell tour," I whisper, and Aunt Mary laughs.

"Your mom told you about that?"

I nod. I know the whole story—how one summer, they charged vacation kids a dollar to take them to the best spots to find pretty shells for souvenirs. They told them what all the shells were called, making up anything they didn't know.

"Those two were something. Always with a plan," Aunt Mary says.

"I heard about the time they bought candy on sale at the grocery store, too. And then walked up and down the beach selling it for twice the cost."

She laughs again. "I don't remember that. Sounds just like them, though. What else has your mom told you about growing up here?"

I hesitate because the true answer is not much. "Well . . . she and Dad used to tell me about the Slow Pitch Social where they met. Dad told me he tried to hit a home run because he wanted to impress Mom and struck out instead."

A little boy rushes in front of us to fill a bucket with ocean water and then lugs it back to where his sisters are working on a sandcastle.

"I'd forgotten about that," Aunt Mary says. "He impressed everybody else, though, diving all over the field making plays and teaching little kids how to throw the ball. He even rode his bike back to pick up an extra gallon of ice cream when they ran out at the Creamery's concession table."

"Really?" I didn't know that part, and I love it. *That's* who Dad is, deep down—the kind of person who picks up extra ice cream and makes friends with little kids.

"Oh, yes. He had a lot of admirers that summer."

"It doesn't still happen, does it?" I ask. "The Slow Pitch Social?"

"Nah. Not in fifteen years, probably. There used to be a field near the center of town—that's where it always was. But a developer bought the land and built houses there. It hasn't happened since."

"I always thought it sounded so fun," I say.

"It was a nice thing," she agrees. "It brought people together, and it was good for local businesses. They all set up tables and sold food. The Creamery table was always the most popular."

We're back to the beach entrance where we started, heading out through the opening in the dunes.

"Hey, what did Danielle mean before?" I ask. "When she said our ice cream orders wouldn't make much of a difference? Is the Creamery in trouble?"

Aunt Mary bends down to pick up somebody's old Ziploc bag that's half buried in the sand. "I hope not. But there's a new ice cream shop that opened up in the spring. Timeless Treats. It's a chain. So far, the Creamery's business is down a lot, and Danielle counts on a big summer." Aunt Mary drops the Ziploc bag in a trash can as we reach the road.

"I doubt Timeless Treats is anywhere as good as the Creamery," I say, and Aunt Mary smiles.

"I'm sure it isn't. Let's hope the novelty wears off soon and everybody goes back to the Creamery."

She leads me over to the park a few blocks away from her house so I can throw. There's a big sandbox, which kind of cracks me up since we're so close to the real thing, and a playground, basketball court, and handball wall. After she makes sure I know how to get back to the house, she says she'll leave me to it and heads off.

The slides and monkey bars are empty, but three kids laugh as they pump themselves higher and higher and then jump off the swings, and a woman rocks a stroller back and forth. Beyond them, there's a man reading a book on a bench under a tree.

I was kind of hoping the park would be empty, but these people are strangers who have every right to be here, not spectators here to judge me if I throw badly. I'll be fine.

I pull my soft, worn glove out of my bag and breathe in the smell of leather, dirt, and sun as I walk to the handball court. I slip my hand inside and grip the cushiony ball in my right hand. There's an oval-shaped mark in the middle of the wall, right around chest-level, where the paint's chipped off. That's where I'll aim.

*Arm back, curl the hand past the ear, pivot, step, let go*, I recite in my head. But my skin gets hot even though the air is cool, and my heartbeat echoes in my eardrums.

I need to get out of my head.

I need to stop thinking and *throw*.

I step in closer to the wall, figuring I'll lob the ball underhand a couple times to warm up. I toss it at the place with the chipped paint, and it bounces back into my glove once, then a second time, and a third. I'm ready, I think.

I back up, squeeze the ball, rotate back and—

"Are you Bea?" someone calls.

I let go all wrong. The ball hits the ground and skitters away.

There's a girl perched on the seat of a green bike. She's about my age, with brown hair peeking out from under her lavender helmet, slightly sunburned white skin, and really blue eyes.

"Hannah, right?" I say. "Hey."

She looks different than I remember, with no glasses and her hair just below her shoulders instead of nearly to her elbows. And she's laughing a little. At me.

I tell myself she's only laughing because it's a funny situation—her startling me right before I let go. She has no idea there's any other reason I'd mess up a simple throw.

She hops off her bike to get the ball, which has rolled all the way to the edge of the basketball court, and she throws it back to me hard, with perfect form.

"I didn't mean to sneak up on you. I passed your aunt

on my way to her house, and she said you were here." She digs into her bag and pulls out a softball glove. "My mom made me bring this in case you wanted to throw together. Do you?"

Do I?

It's such a harmless question. Having a catch with Hannah should be as easy as tying my shoes or walking over to the water fountain near the sandbox and taking a sip.

I don't feel ready. I was counting on throwing by myself. But we both have gloves, and there's *literally* a ball in my hand. How can I say no?

"I don't think I can," I tell her slowly.

Her forehead crinkles. "You don't think you *can*?"

Gran corrects me if I use the word "can" when another verb is more accurate. "Can I use your bathroom?" I asked one time when we were at her apartment for dinner, and she raised her eyebrows and said, "*May* you? Yes. *Can* you? I hope so." Another time, when I said I couldn't leave softball practice early to go with her to a church potluck, she said, "You *can* leave early if you choose. You don't *want* to miss the end of practice, and that's fine as long as you own it."

Right now, though, I literally don't know if I *can* throw the ball with Hannah. I *want* to be able to. But I have no clue what will happen if I try.

A tiny part of me wants to confess what I'm afraid

of. Hannah doesn't know me. I didn't let *her* down at the championships. But it feels like saying it out loud would make it more likely to happen again—like when I can't fall asleep the night before something important, and as soon as I let myself think how bad it'll be if I'm not sleeping soon, *wham*. I'm dooming myself to hours of tossing and turning.

So I tell a white lie instead. "I strained my shoulder a little. I'm sure I'll be fine, but I should probably go easy on it."

Hannah's forehead is still all crinkled, so I don't think she believes me. I need a way out of this awkward moment, and the kids who were on the swings before are racing each other on the monkey bars now. Two of the empty swings are swaying—one side to side, and one back and forth—inviting the next person to hop on.

"Hey, do you want to swing?" I blurt.

Hannah looks at me like I've said the weirdest thing she's ever heard, and honestly maybe I have, but I'm committed to it now. "Come on. It'll be fun!"

I run over to the swings, hoping she'll follow, and take the one on the end. Jessi and I used to race out to the swings at recess in elementary school, but I haven't been on one in ages. I forgot how freeing it feels to pump myself higher and higher. How amazing it is that moving your legs back and forth in the right rhythm is all it takes to fly. Hannah takes her time dragging her bike across the grass, but eventually, she parks it, hooks her helmet around one of the handles, and sits on the swing next to me. She doesn't kick off and start pumping, though. She just draws circles in the dirt with the toes of her sneakers.

I feel silly and a little unfriendly swinging so high above her, so I drag my feet against the ground to slow down. "My mom talks about your mom a lot. She's told me a bunch of stories about stuff they did when they were growing up."

"Oh yeah?" Hannah says. "That surprises me." There's an edge to her voice.

"What do you mean? Why?"

She tips her head back, looking up at the cloudless blue sky instead of answering.

"Because she never comes back here?" I ask.

"Well yeah. And because she wouldn't let us visit."

She looks right at me now, and I have no idea what she's talking about.

"After my parents split up last summer?"

She says it like a question, waiting to see if it'll spark my memory, but I'm lost.

She sighs. "My mom kept promising me we'd do something special after the busy season was over at the

Creamery, and we came up with this idea, to do all this fun stuff in New York City. Hotels were way too expensive, so she called your mom and asked if we could stay at your house since it's pretty close. But your mom said no."

I tighten my grip on the swing's cool metal chain. "Were we busy?"

Hannah shakes her head. "I don't think she gave an excuse. My mom wasn't mad. She said your mom has a complicated relationship with Gray Island and likes to keep the past in the past and we have to respect that. But I thought it was pretty crappy that your mom couldn't do something nice for her friend."

Then she pushes off the ground and starts swinging.

*Mom couldn't do something nice for her friend.*

I picture Danielle this morning—how excited she was to see me. I want to believe there was a good reason Mom couldn't invite them to stay with us—some big deadline or important event. But I think what Danielle said is probably right. Mom doesn't want her Gray Island past to mix with her New Jersey present, ever.

"What position do you play, anyway?" Hannah calls as her swing swoops past me.

It takes me a second to catch up to the subject change. "Oh. I'm a shortstop. You?"

She launches herself off the swing, high into the air, and lands steady on two feet. The little kids who were on the swings before cheer for her, and she does a little curtsy.

Then she turns back to me. "Shortstop," she says.

There's a challenge in her voice. Like she can't wait to get on the field on Monday and show me how good she is.

I am a person who rises to a challenge. Always. But right now, my throat goes tight, and something in my stomach wobbles.

"Look," Hannah says. "My mom wants me to introduce you to people and show you around and all, and that's fine. I can do that. But this camp—it isn't just a fun vacation thing for me. I take softball seriously. This camp's a big opportunity. I need it."

My heart starts beating faster. "It isn't just a fun vacation thing for me, either. I take softball seriously, too. *I* need this camp, too."

For a second, I think she's going to ask me *why* I need the camp, but she just puts her bike helmet back on her head, shrugs, and says, "Okay. I'm gonna go back and help at the Creamery. I'll see you Monday morning."

"See you Monday morning." My voice comes out small, which I *hate*.

I want to say something loud and clear and confident

so Hannah will know who I am and what I'm all about, but she's already pedaling away, slowly at first and then faster once she's back on concrete. She waves to four teenage boys who are shooting baskets on the basketball court.

She thinks I need *her* to show me around and introduce me to people?

She thinks this camp is just some fun thing I signed up for on a whim?

I start pumping myself higher and higher on my swing. When I get so high that I'm even with the bar at the top, I leap off and land at the edge of the dirt, sticking my landing just like Hannah stuck hers.

I glance over at those kids to see if they'll clap for me, too, but they're not paying attention.

Whatever.

I pick up my glove and the cushiony softball and jog over to the handball court. In my head, I hear Hannah laughing when I threw the ball away and saying *she* takes softball seriously.

As if I don't?

As if I don't need this softball camp more than anyone else possibly could?

I hurl the ball at the wall, hard, and it smacks the spot with the chipped-off paint and rolls back to me. I pick it up and throw it again and again and again, each throw hitting the mark I'm aiming for, practically cracking the cement, I bet, because I'm throwing so freaking hard.

The basketball guys stop bouncing their ball. "Hey! What did that wall do to you?" one of them calls.

I freeze because my arm muscles aren't loose yet. I shouldn't be throwing this hard—I could strain something for real.

But I threw the ball right where I wanted to. No brain glitch, no panicking. No doubting myself.

There is no way Hannah's a better shortstop than I am, and I can't wait to prove that to her.

# CHAPTER 10

On Monday morning, Aunt Mary pulls into the entrance of Gray Island Academy. The sign out front says, "A preparatory boarding and day school for students in grades 6–12."

"Here we are!" she tells me.

And I don't know what this school is preparing kids in grades 6–12 *for* but it's got to be something great, because this place is amazing. The campus is hilly and sprawling with large stone buildings and pastel hydrangeas blooming everywhere. We pass a soccer field, another building, and a track, following the signs for "Rose Marvin's Passion and Performance Softball Camp." And then there it is: the softball field.

It's nicer than any other field I've ever played on except this one time when Dad convinced a grounds-crew guy to let Jessi and me throw the ball around on the game field at Princeton. But this one is just as nice as that. The emerald green grass in the outfield is mown into criss-cross patterns. There are fresh, bright white lines along the base paths, and the infield dirt looks like the grounds crew at Yankee Stadium just raked it during the seventh inning stretch.

"Wow," I say.

"I bet you'll have to walk around the grassy part putting back any divots you kick up. That's what they make the kids do after soccer games."

I laugh, but Aunt Mary doesn't.

"I mean it. I watched a game here once and all the players lined up and walked across the field when it was over, pressing tufts of grass back down." She shrugs. "I get frustrated that this place has so many more resources than the other island schools. But I shouldn't criticize. It's good to take care of nice things."

She tells me to have a great day, and I thank her for the ride and then hop out of the car, imagining the perfect, predictable hops the ball's going to take on this perfect, beautiful field.

A teenage girl wearing a Gray Island Academy softball T-shirt calls me over so she can check me in, and it takes her a while to find my name on the list. It should be near the top, under B for Bartlett. Instead it's scrawled in at the bottom, but whatever—it's there. The girl hands me a welcome bag with a Passion and Performance water bottle, a schedule, and a list of rules, and she tells me to find a seat anywhere on the bleachers. I glance through the paperwork as I walk over. There are themes and special speakers on some of the days. Conditioning. Baserunning. Mindfulness. Stats and Scorekeeping. Camp championship. My heart rate spikes just seeing the word "championship," but I breathe in and out until it slows back down.

Hannah's sitting with a few other people at the top of the bleachers, but I don't need her to introduce me to anyone. I'm thinking I might just sit by myself, until a girl in the front waves. I think she's Asian American, and she's wearing a University of Connecticut sweatshirt and has her hair in two French braids.

"Hey there!" she says. "Come sit with us!"

As soon as my butt hits the metal, she launches into introductions. "Okay, yay! So, I'm Emery. And this beautiful buttercup is my summer sister, Izzy." She pauses to point to the girl next to her, who has pale white skin and hair that's dyed pink but fading back to blondish. "And that's our new friend Nia on the end!" Nia, who's wearing a Gray Island Academy basketball T-shirt and has light brown skin and hair pulled into a tight, high bun, smiles at me.

"Our families come to Gray Island every year," Izzy explains. "Hence the summer sister thing. And this year Emery thinks we need to branch out and make new friends. Hence the aggressively flagging people down to sit with us."

Izzy's the only person here who doesn't look ready to play softball. She's wearing denim cutoffs and a fitted black T-shirt.

Emery fake pouts. "Dude. That was called being *friendly*. Maybe you've heard of it?"

"You're being so *friendly* you haven't asked the person you're befriending what her name is," Izzy points out.

"Oops!" Emery laughs. "What's your name, person we're befriending?"

"I'm Bea."

"Bea! Short for Beatrice or Beatrix or nothing?" Emery asks.

"Um, Beatrix. But I really just go by Bea."

Emery nods. "Noted. Nia goes to school here. Isn't she lucky?"

Nia starts explaining how she's a day student, which means she lives here on Gray Island with her family and doesn't stay in the dorms the way the kids who live on the mainland do, and Emery asks a bunch of questions about Gray Island in the winter, since her family only comes in the summer, and then her eyes go wide and she squeals. "Look look look!"

I follow her gaze, and there is Rose Marvin, in person, walking over to the front of the bleachers with the other coaches. She wears her light brown hair in her trademark ponytail braid, which bounces over the back strap of her white Nike visor. She isn't tall for a softball player, but she *seems* tall because of how she carries herself, and being this close to her makes me sit up straighter.

She sits on a folding chair next to the other two coaches—a young woman with tan skin, short hair, and a Gray Island Academy softball T-shirt, and a man who looks about my parents' age, with hair that's halfway between blond and silver, rosy white skin, and a dark green polo shirt.

Once the rest of the twenty-five campers are here, the man gets up and introduces himself as Bill Conway, the high school varsity coach at Gray Island Academy.

"On behalf of the Academy, I want to welcome all of you. We're very glad to have you here on campus for the next two weeks."

He reads us the Gray Island Academy Athletic Department's Mission Statement, which has a bunch of stuff about sportsmanship and leadership and positive competition. Mom would be a fan, since it covers most of the stuff she's always emphasizing to me about sports, except Mom would half-jokingly suggest it should be "sports-personship" instead of sportsmanship. She always points out the sexism in sports terms, especially baseball and softball positions. At home, Jessi and I used to push for everybody to say stuff like "first baseperson" or just "first base" instead of "first baseman," but we kind of gave up after a while.

When Coach Conway finishes reading the statement, he says, "I'm delighted to get to know you all and thrilled that you're spending part of your summer with us."

It's a little cheesy, but he says it like he means it, and I can tell he's the kind of coach who likes the players at least as much as he likes the sport. He introduces the other coach, Gabby Flores, who played Division 1 softball in college and coaches the JV team here at the Academy.

And then he says, "Without further ado, it's my pleasure to introduce one of our most accomplished Gray Island Academy alums and the most outstanding player I've ever had the honor of coaching. The one and only Rose Marvin!"

Everyone cheers as Rose jogs over.

"Thank you so much, everybody!" Rose says. "It's good to be back home on Gray Island. Let's get to know each other a little bit and then get to work!"

She has us all sit in a big circle on the bright green

outfield grass. I end up between Emery and Nia and across the circle from Hannah, who gives me a quick nod.

"So again, welcome!" Rose says, and I kind of can't believe that the same Rose Marvin who's on that poster in my bedroom at home is *here*, sitting crisscross applesauce in the grass. "You can call me Rose. Or Coach Rose, if you prefer. I'm so excited to get to know you all this week. Let's go around and introduce ourselves. Sound good?"

"Sounds great!" Emery says.

"Simmer down there, Lau," Izzy whispers, and Emery reaches over to swat her arm with the outside of one hand.

"Who wants to go first?" Coach Rose asks.

I raise my hand because I want to make a good impression as quickly as possible, but Hannah calls out, "I'll go!" and Coach Rose beams.

"Great! Thank you for being brave."

Hannah beams back.

*Ugh.*

"I'm Hannah Rogers," she says. "I use she/her pronouns, I go to Gray Island Middle, and I'm a shortstop." Then she pauses. "Is there anything else you want me to say?"

"Not necessarily," Coach Rose replies. "Unless you want to tell us any specific goals you have for our next two weeks together?"

"Well, to be totally honest, my plan is to impress Coach Conway so much he gives me an athletic scholarship to Gray Island Academy just like you had for high school."

Coach Conway laughs, but I don't think Hannah was joking.

"Well, that's quite a goal, Hannah," Rose says. "I respect your boldness."

Hannah's sitting next to a pretty Black girl with long braids gathered in a ponytail. Once everyone settles down, she goes next and says her name is Tasha.

"I play center field, mostly. And I want to learn to bunt better, since this one yells at me every time I strike out."

She elbows Hannah, who shrugs. "She's so fast! She should be getting on base any way she can!"

We keep going around the circle, and everybody lives here on the island until we get to Izzy, who says she's from New York City and doesn't really have a position.

"I put right field on my form as my position because Emery says that's the best place to stick somebody who doesn't know what they're doing," she says. "But mostly I'm just here because Em's obsessed with softball and we always do camps together while we're here for the summer. I was hoping we'd do theater camp this week."

"We'll see if we can win you over to softball, Izzy," Coach

Rose says, and then Emery tells us all she's from Connecti-cut, and she plays first base.

"And I'm super excited to be here and I just want to soak up whatever you have to teach us, Coach Rose, because softball's pretty much my life and you're pretty much my hero!"

Hannah rolls her eyes, but I like that Emery doesn't tone down how excited she is.

Coach Rose turns to me next, and even though we're literally going around the circle in order and I knew I was next, I'm flustered.

"Oh! Um, well, I'm Bea. She/her pronouns. I'm from New Jersey, and I'm a shortstop."

Everybody's looking at me, and I want to show them that I care about softball at least as much as Hannah or Emery or anyone else, but I can't think of a good way to say that. So I just tell everyone I'm happy to be here, too, and leave it at that.

I'll make *my* statements on the field.

After introductions, we pair up for warm-up catches. I throw with Nia, who's also a shortstop, and we're next to Emery and Izzy.

Izzy keeps complaining about how big the softball is

and how hard it is to throw, and Emery chatters away. I'm grateful for the distractions, because I'm basically on autopilot as Nia and I throw the ball back and forth, and I feel more and more like myself each time the ball hits her glove.

Next, we split up by positions. Pitchers and catchers go with Coach Flores, outfielders go with Coach Conway, and infielders go with Coach Rose.

"Hmm, I thought there were two of you at each infield position," Rose says, flipping through some pages on her clipboard and looking from Hannah to Nia to me. "But I guess there are three shortstops, huh?"

"We probably *had* two," Hannah says. "Bea was a last-minute addition."

And that's true, technically, but I don't think there was a limit on how many shortstops could sign up. The person on the phone who said I could still register didn't even ask my position.

"Well, no problem," Rose says. "The three of you can take turns at short for now."

"What about when we split into teams?" Hannah presses. "Because if one of the teams has two shortstops and the other team only has one, the playing time won't be even."

"Let's not worry about that yet. I'll figure out how to

handle teams, okay?" Rose walks to the side of the field to grab her bat, and I glare at Hannah as we walk out to shortstop.

"Why did you say all that?" I ask her.

"I told you, this camp is important to me. I want to make sure I get playing time when it counts, that's all."

Her voice is super calm, but every calm feeling leaves my body.

"I have as much of a right to be here as anybody else," I tell her. "I want playing time when it counts, too."

Hannah shrugs but doesn't say anything, and that shrug makes me want to scream.

"I'm sure the coaches will figure out how to make things fair," Nia says.

Before Hannah can respond, Rose walks back to home plate with a bat and a bucket of balls. "All right. Everybody just throw to first base to start. Stay where you are for one full time around the infield, then rotate behind the other person . . ." She pauses to look over at the three of us at short. "Or other *people* at your position."

She hits an easy grounder to Emery, who fields it cleanly and jogs back a few feet to step on first base. A girl named Melanie, who's lined up at second base, is next, and she's a little tentative—she stays back on her heels and waits for the ball to come to her instead of moving toward it—but she picks it up without a problem and tosses it to Emery at first. Then it's Hannah's turn.

Hannah charges, snatches the ball on a bounce, and throws it hard and on target. She gives me an infuriating little nod when she passes me to move to the back of the line of shortstops, and then I'm up, waiting for my turn. I crouch down into fielding position and pound my fist into my glove, watching the other players field their grounders.

When Rose hits the ball to me, I charge and pick it up, just as confident and clean as Hannah. My throw is on target, too, and hard. Harder than Hannah's, I'm pretty sure.

Adrenaline courses through my body as I jog to the back of the line. *Good* adrenaline. The kind that makes me feel like I can get to any ball and make any play, not the kind that leaves me shaky and panicked.

We keep going, fielding and throwing, fielding and throwing. Nia's a decent shortstop, too, but not as strong as me or Hannah. She's a really good athlete, but she told Emery, Izzy, and me that basketball's her main sport, and I'm guessing she hasn't been playing softball for that long.

Hannah's at least four inches taller than I am, with super long arms and legs, which means she can get to everything. When we start practicing turning double plays, Rose smacks a grounder in the gap toward third base—far enough that I'd dive for it if I were the one fielding—but

Hannah doesn't leave her feet. Her reach is so long that she shifts, extends her arm, and she's got it. And her throw to second is quick and accurate.

"Nice range!" Rose calls, and Hannah grins.

But whatever. She has extremely long limbs, so she can reach extremely far. That's all.

I take her place and get into position, shifting to cover second base when Rose hits to Emery and then Melanie, fielding their throws and firing to first after each one. And then it's my turn for a grounder at short, and for a second I'm nervous. Will Rose hit a ball that pulls me toward third base like she did with Hannah to test whether my range is as good as hers?

But she hits the ball short instead, so I have to charge. *Show her up*, I tell myself. *Be better than Hannah. Beat Hannah!*

I barehand the ball instead of picking it up with my glove, and whip a throw to second.

Melanie gasps as the ball smacks her glove. She stares at her hand for a second before she regroups and throws to first.

Rose whistles. "Barehanded! That was gutsy!"

Now it's my turn to grin.

Dad sometimes talks about finding a focusing phrase. Something short and clear to set your intention. To help you concentrate on what you need to do. He had Jessi repeat to herself "seams or leather, seams or leather" every time she went up to bat when she was in a slump so she'd watch the ball all the way in—so closely that she'd be able to tell which part of the ball she'd made contact with. When I was swinging and missing at too many pitches that were up at my shoulders, he had me repeat, "Wait for your pitch. Wait for your pitch," so I'd remember to be choosy.

*Beat Hannah.*

It's not the most sportspersonlike goal I could come up with, but it's going to work if I start to freak out again—I can tell.

Because if I stay focused on beating Hannah, I won't have to worry about coming apart at the seams and beating myself.

CHAPTER

11

When we get back to the house at the end of the day, I'm a little hungry, but I don't stop to eat the snack Aunt Mary offers me. I go straight to the bedroom to FaceTime Mom and Dad, because I promised I'd call as soon as camp was done. The phone doesn't even ring one full time before they're on, their faces crowding together in the frame.

"Bea! How are you, honey?" Mom asks.

"How'd it go?" Dad says at the same time.

I laugh. "It was great."

"Oh, wonderful!" Mom says, and even though Dad's eyes look tired and his face is pale, his smile stretches so wide that the corners of his mouth nearly reach his earlobes.

They adjust the phone, and I can see they're at the kitchen table. There's Mom's favorite dogwood tree out the window behind them and the edge of our whiteboard family calendar on the wall.

"No issues on the field?" Dad asks.

"No issues. I think throwing against a wall with that training softball really helped."

"Oh, Bumble. That's the best news," he says. "I'm so happy."

And in this moment, he *looks* happy. Truly happy. Before-everyone-found-out-what-he-did happy.

"I talked to Danielle," Mom says. "She said Hannah's at the camp, too?"

I don't want to ruin this moment by asking why Mom said no when Danielle wanted to visit, so I just say, "Yep. She plays shortstop, too. She's good."

And I try not to think too hard about what Mom would say if she knew my new focusing phrase.

Mom's number one rule for softball is that she wants it to bring out the best in me. She wants me to be a good teammate. To compete in *positive* ways and lift other girls up, not tear them down. She used to be a runner and she got a track scholarship to college and everything. But she says it was a toxic team environment in college. The coaches would pit people against each other. She never loved running the way I love softball, and she disliked it more and more the longer she ran on that team, but she

119

couldn't quit without losing her scholarship. She wants to make sure I never have an experience like that with sports.

I change the subject. "How was the open house yesterday?"

Mom and Dad exchange a look, and my heart sinks.

"Did someone put in an offer already?"

They warned me before I left home that Rina the Realtor said our house could sell really quickly. She'd sold some other homes in our area before the open house was over. I know that's what we need—a quick sale. But I hate the idea of driving by our house the way we sometimes drive by the house where Gran and Gramps used to live. Noticing the ugly color the new owners repainted the shutters, or the way they let the garden grow wild. Wondering who's sleeping in *my* bedroom and using the icemaker in the brand-new fridge we only bought last year. I'm not ready.

"No. Not yet. But we only just listed it," Mom says. "These things take time."

"Oh. Okay." I let out a big breath. "I thought you said places are selling super fast?"

Mom shakes her head. "Sometimes. More often it takes a while."

"We were hoping for a walk-off home run, but we need to play small ball," Dad chimes in. "But some lucky family will snap it up soon."

When Dad uses softball metaphors, Mom usually laughs or rolls her eyes in a way that's affectionate, not annoyed. But right now, she doesn't crack a smile. She closes her eyes as if she's searching behind her eyelids for some patience and breathes. *I'm calm and in control, I'm calm and in control*, she's probably telling herself inside her head. Is she searching for some patience to deal with *Dad*?

"You keep on crushing it on the softball field," Dad tells me. "We'll hold down the fort and keep you updated on the house. Sound good?"

I swallow. "Sounds good."

"We're so proud of you, Bea," Mom says, and now her eyes are open and she looks like her regular self again.

I promise to call again after camp tomorrow, and we say I love you and hang up. There's a text from Jessi saying she and Emilia went to a movie because it was too hot to be outside and asking what I did today, but I don't know how to respond without lying. So I dismiss it for now, promising myself I'll tell her about camp later, and I go down to the kitchen, where Aunt Mary's frowning into a salad bowl.

I eat the banana and trail mix she set out for me and ask, "Everything okay?"

"I'm not entirely sure," she says. "This doesn't look like the picture on the recipe."

She holds up a printed-out recipe with a picture of a colorful "summer kale salad," and she's right that what's in her salad bowl bears zero resemblance.

She used arugula or something instead of kale and a whole lot more cherry tomatoes than there are in the photo. Her salad is swimming in dressing, and most of the goat cheese she tried to mix in is stuck to the spoon.

"I'm sure it'll still taste good," I say, but she raises her eyebrows.

"I don't know, Bea. You suffered through that stir-fry last night. You should know that isn't a given."

I burst out laughing even though I don't mean to. "No! It . . . it's really nice of you to cook for me. And maybe the lettuce you used just didn't soak up as much dressing as the kale would have? My mom says kale-based salads need more dressing. Maybe we could add more lettuce if you have some?"

"Brilliant!" She finds some baby spinach in the fridge, and then says, "Linda's a pretty gourmet cook, so I was relegated to dishwashing duty for many years. Now that I cook for myself, I eat a lot of frozen dinners and pasta."

"I really like pasta," I offer. "It's fine with me if we just have that."

She smiles. "Luckily, I'm also an excellent grill master, and I'm planning to grill the rest of the meal tonight. So we should be safe."

I take charge of adding some spinach to absorb the dressing, and Aunt Mary gets the grill going outside.

"What can I do next?" I ask when she comes back in.

She hands me an ear of corn and I start to pull off the papery green leaves, one layer at a time. Mom always pulls back the top of each husk at the grocery store to make sure she's choosing good ones. These husks are all closed up, but each one has row after row of even, sunshine yellow kernels.

I think of Xander and that yellow "you are my sunshine" shirt, and it hits me like a line drive to the gut: how he liked me and I liked him and we were on the brink of something, and then we weren't.

But I banish the memory of yellow-shirt-wearing Xander and pluck a stringy bit out from in between rows of corn.

Aunt Mary grills the corn along with some salmon, and then we set the table on the deck to eat out there.

She closes her eyes and mouths something before she picks up her fork to eat. I noticed her doing the same thing yesterday.

"Are you saying grace?" I ask. "I can do it with you, if you want. We do at home sometimes."

"I'm not praying, exactly," she says. "But I am giving thanks, I suppose. I have a type of arthritis that causes me a lot of pain some of the time, mostly in my knees. So on the good days, I try to take a moment to say I'm grateful to my legs for supporting my weight and getting me where I wanted to go without any pain all day long. It's a little goofy."

"I don't think it's goofy," I tell her. "I like it."

It reminds me of the way Mom sometimes says, "Your body is an instrument, not an ornament." She wants me to focus on what my body can *do*, not what it looks like.

I take a second to feel grateful to my body, too—all the muscles and bones and joints in my arms, legs, back, and hands that worked together today each time I ran and threw and hit. And to my brain, since it didn't glitch or spiral.

"That stinks about your arthritis," I tell Aunt Mary.

"It sure does," she replies. "But for now, cheers to good days. Seems like you had one, too?"

"Definitely. Cheers to good days," I echo, and we clink our water glasses.

The renters pass by on their way out to a restaurant in town for dinner, and a bunch of Aunt Mary's neighbors who are out for evening walks stop to say hi. There's a white-haired older couple Aunt Mary calls Mr. and Mrs. Anderson even though she's a grown-up herself, and they tell me they've lived in the tiny house across the street since before Aunt Mary and my mom were born. There's a woman named Aruni, who Aunt Mary says is in her book club, and then there's a family with two little kids. They live in the house where Danielle grew up, Aunt Mary explains as they go by.

After the last neighbors pass, everything's quiet except for the chirp of crickets and the distant swish of the ocean. As I eat the last bites of my grilled salmon and buttery corn, I'm thinking about Mom—how she grew up in this house, probably ate dinner on this deck. How she would know most of these people here, too, the same way Dad always knows everyone in Butler, except she never wants to come back.

"What's on your mind?" Aunt Mary asks. "If you want to talk about it, that is."

I hesitate for a second, and then blurt out, "Hannah said something to me. About how Danielle asked my mom if the two of them could stay at our house last year and Mom said no. Danielle told Hannah that Mom likes to keep everything from Gray Island in the past."

I guess I'm sort of lobbing the statement out there like

an easy pitch down the middle of the plate, just in case Aunt Mary wants to swing. Just in case she might tell me something Mom hasn't.

She rests her fork on the edge of her mostly empty plate and says, "Do you know those baby gates people set up on their stairs sometimes? To block them off, so little kids don't fall?"

I nod, but I have no clue where she's going with this.

"Bear with me. I hope this is going to make sense. My ex, Linda—her sister had those up in her house when her kids were little. I helped install them. The idea with those gates is, you need them for a while, but once the kids are big enough and stairs aren't so scary, you take them down. Right?"

"Right."

"So your mom . . . after our mother died and then Evan died a few years later, your mom needed to set up some gates around the island to protect herself. And with good reason. She's opened them up a couple times since, but she hasn't taken them down yet."

My heart speeds up. I know almost nothing about Mom's mother except that she was a teacher, like Aunt Mary, and she had an aneurysm and died young— when Mom was in her twenties and living in Boston.

But the way Aunt Mary says, "after our mother died and then Evan died" makes me realize: Evan must have been from Gray Island.

I assumed he and Mom had met in Boston, because everything Mom's told me about him happened there. He played the saxophone in an orchestra there and taught music lessons to kids. He loved basketball, and they went to Celtics games every once in a while, when Mom's grad school professor gave them tickets. And sometimes they'd go to a park outside the city on the weekends, where Evan sketched birds while Mom wrote stories in a notebook.

But he must be from here, not Boston, because why else would his death have anything to do with Mom putting gates up around Gray Island? Was *he* the boyfriend Mom was with during the summer Dad tried to impress her at the Slow Pitch Social?

I try to fit this new piece of information in with the pieces I already knew about Evan, but I know so little, really. He liked brownies. He refused to call their landlord when they had a mouse problem in their apartment because he couldn't bear the idea that the landlord might use traps that would kill the mice. He was sick and then he got better and then he got worse, and he died. He liked spy novels and sci-fi movies and jazz. That's pretty much all I know.

"Where did Evan grow up?" I ask, testing out my new theory. "In this neighborhood?"

Aunt Mary shakes her head. "Closer to town. His family didn't live on the island for long. They moved here when he and your mom were in high school, and his parents moved away years ago. They retired to Florida, I think. But he's still a part of this place for your mom, and everybody here knew them together and knows what happened."

"They know how he got sick, you mean?" I say, and she blinks a little strangely, but then she nods.

"Right. Anyway. I'm hoping that, eventually, your mom might be ready to take the gates down. And I think having you come for a visit is a good step. And investing in the cottage renovation, too, and helping me make decisions about the design. That meant a lot, that she wanted to be involved."

She stands and picks up her plate and glass.

"It's getting chilly. Shall we head back in?"

I want her to keep talking about Evan and Mom, but I think she's finished now, and it really *is* cold. Goose bumps cover my arms.

I follow her inside the house, and once the dishes are loaded into the dishwasher, she says, "What would you like to do now? Watch some TV? Play a board game? Do some art?"

"Wait . . . some art?" I ask.

"Sure. Do you like art?"

I shake my head. "I'm, like, the least artistic person ever."

"Ah, I doubt that's true."

"No, seriously. Art is the only class I've never gotten an A in. I can barely draw a stick figure."

Aunt Mary raises her eyebrows. "Well, how would you like to join me for my summer challenge?"

She explains that the last couple of summers, ever since she and Linda broke up and her arthritis flares got more frequent and made it harder to travel on her own, she's assigned herself a challenge. Last summer, she learned to knit and crochet. The summer before, she took ukulele lessons.

"I think it makes me a better teacher, getting an annual reminder of what it feels like to learn something new. Although maybe I should have picked cooking this year, huh?" She winks at me. "But I went with art. I'm taking two different classes at the community center in July. But for now, I do these directed drawings my students turned me onto. Want to try?"

"Sure, I'll try," I say, because it seems rude to refuse. "But I'm warning you. I'm *really* bad at art."

She just shrugs. "I'll bet you might surprise yourself."

She gets her laptop and pulls up a YouTube channel with instruction videos for drawing all sorts of things—a narwhal, a chameleon, a cute penguin. Jessi and some of my other friends used to watch videos like these to learn how to draw the characters from books they liked when we were younger, but I never got into them. Eventually, Aunt Mary finds one for a softball player.

The screenshot of the finished picture looks way beyond anything I'm capable of, but Aunt Mary and I sit at her kitchen table with paper and pencils and follow along as the person who made the video goes step-by-step, adding circles, curves, lines—all these tiny, manageable pieces that come together to create something pretty impressive.

Aunt Mary takes out a few Sharpies and a big box of crayons like the one I had as a kid, and we trace over the pencil lines of our drawings with markers and then color everything in. It's relaxing and satisfying and *fun*.

"That wasn't so painful, was it?" she asks when we finish.

"I liked it," I admit, and she grins.

"I'm glad you gave it a chance."

After we say good night, I pin my drawing up on the bulletin board in the room where I'm staying.

It's not like I think I'm an artist all of a sudden. All I did was follow someone else's instructions. But this piece of paper was completely blank, and now there's a softball player on it. My hand made all those marks and shaded in all those colors, one step at a time.

# CHAPTER 12

The next morning at camp, Emery waves me over to join her and Izzy.

"Izzy needs extra throwing practice," she says. "Want to help?"

"*Needs* is a strong word," Izzy huffs. "And I'm doing what you said. It's not my fault my fingers are small and the ball's enormous. It keeps falling out of my hand!"

"Let me see," I say.

I watch as Izzy tries to throw the ball to Emery. Her form is better than it was yesterday. She's rotating and stepping with her opposite foot, which is a good start. But the ball still dives out of her hand and hits the ground a few feet in front of her.

"Can you show me how you're holding it?" I ask, and when she picks up the ball, I see the problem. She has it cupped too far back in her palm.

I pick up another ball and show her the right way to grip it—with the pads of my four fingers across the seam and my thumb loosely against the bottom. "Like a kickstand on a bike," Dad used to say. Just for balance.

"Now it *really* feels like it'll slip right out," she says.

I get what she means, because in that directed drawing video last night, the teacher said to make sure you're not throttling your pencil. She said you have more control if you grip the pencil loosely, which felt all wrong to me at first, but it worked. Holding a softball's kind of the same thing.

"It might feel weird until you're used to it," I tell Izzy. "But if you squeeze the ball too tight, it doesn't spin right."

Izzy doesn't look convinced, but she tries anyway, and this time her throw's better. It's soft and a little floaty, but it spins the way it should. Emery reaches out to catch it and then cheers.

"Iz!" she shouts. "That was so good!"

"It was *not* so good," Izzy says. "It just wasn't completely awful." But her cheeks turn a little bit pink, and she's biting back a smile.

She throws two good ones in a row, and then the next one really does slip out of her hand when she pulls her arm back, but no one gets worked up. She just picks it up and tries again. I'm a little jealous of her—to be so new at softball that any progress she makes is obvious and there's no pressure to be great.

After we warm up, we're split into two groups to cycle through morning activities. My group goes with Rose for fielding and baserunning work, and Hannah's in the other group, which stays with Coach Conway for a hitting clinic first. Then the groups switch.

Every once in a while, my mind drifts back toward the terrible championships, and I worry I'll let go of the ball too early or too late. But each time, I fight off my panic by watching Hannah—noticing how well she does and willing myself to do better.

I keep focusing on beating Hannah all day Wednesday, too, when a hitting coach comes and we do all sorts of drills at the plate, and then on Thursday, when the focus is on baserunning and sliding. We do conditioning at the end of the day, and I go all out on every sprint. I'm beating everybody except Tasha, who freaking *flies*, over and over. But by the end, I'm getting tired. I'm pretty sure Hannah's gaining on me, so I cut a couple of sprints a teeny bit short, tapping the ground just in front of the line we're running toward instead of making it all the way there. But it isn't an official race or anything. Everybody does that kind of thing.

When we're finally done running, Coach Conway comes over to compliment my hustle. "You're definitely your mom's kid, sprinting like that," he says, and I pause with my water bottle halfway to my mouth.

"You know my mom?"

"Christina Westover, right? We grew up together. I saw you were a last-minute add and wondered what your connection to the island was, and then I recognized her name on your paperwork. Tell her I said hi if you think of it."

I thank him and bend down to take off my sweaty cleats, but then Rose calls my name and I straighten back up. I'm smiling as I jog over, ready for her to compliment my hustle, too.

But what she says is, "Make sure you get all the way to the line on those sprints next time. I know you're a competitive player, and that competitiveness serves you well. But it can hold you back, too. Don't cut corners, okay?"

The smile slides off my face and my stomach twists. "Okay. I'll make sure I touch the line on every sprint next time."

My voice sounds calm, but I don't feel calm at all. Rose thinks I cut corners. Does she think I'm being too competitive with Hannah, too?

I'm tense and shaky as I walk over to the bench to get my bag, and when I look at my phone, there's yet another text from Jessi asking how my vacation's going and telling me to send a beach picture since she's stuck at home.

And—my heart accelerates—there's also a text from *Xander*.

*Hey.*

That's all he wrote. One measly word.

What the heck does that mean? What am I supposed to do with *hey*?

I delete Xander's message and text Jessi a quick, *Vacation's great! Miss you! I'll send a beach pic later. Let's talk soon!*

Then I take off for Aunt Mary's car before waiting to see if Jessi replies.

When I get back to Aunt Mary's house, I try calling Dad's phone, but he doesn't pick up, so I FaceTime Mom instead.

She's sitting at the kitchen table again when she answers, but there's no Dad in sight, and this time the family whiteboard calendar isn't on the wall behind her. There's a random painting of flowers, and I kind of hate it.

"Hey there, honey!" Mom says.

"Hi! Um, where's Dad?"

She glues on a smile and tells me in a too-cheerful voice that Rina the Realtor suggested they clear out some clutter to "stage" the house for more showings over the weekend.

"Rina thinks if we can make the house look less obviously *ours*, it'll be easier for other people to imagine it as *theirs*. So Dad loaded up the car with some things we don't need and took it to Uncle Andy's to store it in their basement for now, since we want to keep our basement tidy."

That explains the missing whiteboard. What else was too obviously *ours* to get to stay? My softball trophies? The photos on the Wall of Bea?

She asks about camp, so I tell her the part about Coach Conway saying I run like her and try to ignore the way my stomach squirms as I skip the stuff Rose said and the way I keep measuring myself up against Hannah.

"How's Dad doing?" I ask, and she hesitates just a second before saying, "It's good for him to have a project. Staging the house is keeping him busy."

Since he doesn't have a *job* to keep him busy.

"And how are you?"

"Oh, you know," she says, but I *don't* know.

She talks about the article she's working on and a podcast interview she did this morning and how she saw one of my teachers at the grocery store. But she doesn't tell me how she *feels*. And suddenly it makes me kind of mad that she has all these baby gates up all the time.

"Why did you tell Danielle and Hannah they couldn't stay at our house last year?" I blurt, and Mom's eyes go wide. "Hannah told me about it. She thought it was crappy that you wouldn't let them come."

There's an unfamiliar kind of adrenaline bubbling through me because I do *not* talk to my mom like this. I shouldn't be talking to her like this. But also: I *did*. And I'm still here and she's still there, and she hasn't even scolded me for using the word "crappy."

"I can see how Hannah would feel that way," she says, finally. "It was right after your school year started, and things were hectic. But I've felt funny about saying no ever since. Danielle's always been a good friend to me. I should have been a better friend to her."

"Oh." I'm surprised she actually answered my question, especially when I asked it rudely. I guess I figure I'm on a roll and I might as well keep asking her things, so I say, "Are you mad? At Dad, I mean. For what he did."

Mom lets out a long breath in a hiss. "Oh, Bea. I'm not . . ." She shakes her head. "I can't go down that road, honey. What's done is done, and I've got to keep moving forward."

I wait to feel relieved because that's *good* she isn't mad. It's good she's moving forward, managing the situation, being Dad's teammate, like always. But for some reason I feel worse than I did before she answered my question, not better.

Her phone dings with a notification and she sighs and says she has a work call in a few minutes. "Unless you need to talk more. I can text right now and push it off if you need me to."

But I tell her that I'm fine and she should go ahead and take the call.

"I'm so proud of you, Bumble," she says before she goes. "For asking for what you needed and taking this trip. I love you, my strong, brave girl."

I tell her I love her, too, but when I end the call, I *feel* it, all of a sudden, how far away from my parents I am right now. An ocean separates us, and a bunch of states, too. That distance makes my heart ache.

And I don't think Mom would be proud of me if she knew how Rose scolded me at the end of camp today for cutting corners. I know she wouldn't be proud of me if she knew I still haven't told Jessi I'm not doing the sleepaway camp in Virginia with her. I need to talk to Jessi for real. It just . . . hurts too much, thinking about how nervous and judgy Jessi sounded when she tried to talk to me about Dad after everyone found out what happened. Even though Dad took her on all those surprise adventures. Even though he taught her to throw a softball and play all our favorite card games back when her brothers were born really premature and she spent so much time at our house while her parents were going back and forth to the hospital. She should know he's a good person who was in a bad situation. She should be on his side, but it doesn't feel like she is. Every time I try to make myself call her, I just *can't*.

Aunt Mary comes in to ask if spaghetti's good for dinner, but when she sees the look on my face, she stops.

"You okay?"

"Yes," I say. "Maybe. I don't know. I miss my parents. And I hate that we have to move out of our house. And Rose sort of criticized me today. For not running all the way to the line when we were doing sprints. I'm worried she thinks I'm a cheater. And I don't know how to talk to my best friend, so I keep blowing her off."

Aunt Mary sits down next to me on the edge of the bed. "That's a lot," she says. "Sometimes when I'm dealing with a lot, it helps to put my hand on my heart, close my eyes, and tell myself, *This feels hard because it* is *hard. I'm doing my best.*"

She demonstrates and then looks at me like she's waiting to see if I'll do it, too, but that is one goofy Aunt Mary thing I have no desire to try.

"The beach helps, also," she adds. "What would you say to a sunset beach picnic?"

And maybe I *am* an ocean girl like she said before, because it sounds pretty great to be by the water where the swishing waves might drown out the thoughts in my head. It sounds way better than the hand-on-heart thing, anyway.

CHAPTER

13

We pick up takeout from Aunt Mary's favorite seafood shack and drive to the westernmost part of the island, where she says the sunsets are the prettiest.

She parks on the side of the road, right up against the dunes. It's late enough that the lifeguards are off duty and most people have gone home. There's a mom pulling a wagon full of beach stuff, trailed by two kids with salty-wet hair and boogie boards dangling over their shoulders.

A couple of teenagers lock up their bikes and walk onto the beach. An older couple around Gran's age follows them, holding sun-faded folding chairs and a red-and-white cooler like the one Dad packs food in when I have away games.

We grab folding chairs from Aunt Mary's trunk, and I slide off my sandals and carry them in my hand. My leg muscles are tired and achy from running so hard at camp, but I like the way my feet sink into the soft, cool sand.

Wind whips my hair all around my face, and choppy, gray-blue waves crash against the shore and roll back out to sea. Seagulls flit around, searching the sand for food, and my head is clearer out here on the beach. The crisp, salty air filters out some of the feelings that started to overwhelm me before.

I'll be better tomorrow, I promise myself. I won't cut any corners on the field. I'll tell Jessi the truth. She'll still have Emilia and Monique with her at sleepaway camp, and she gets along with everybody. I'm sure she'll be fine making friends with a random roommate.

We set up our chairs and sit down to eat our dinner while we watch the waves crash onto the shore. The sky was blue earlier today, but it isn't anymore. It's on its way to pink or maybe orange, but it isn't there yet. Right now, it isn't any color I can name, and the clouds stretch out long and thin above the horizon.

We unwrap our food, and Aunt Mary closes her eyes to mouth something. Appreciation for another good day, I think.

I take a tiny bite of my lobster roll, which I got because Aunt Mary recommended it even though I'm not positive I'll like it. It's delicious, though. Creamy and salty and crunchy, too.

"What happens when it isn't a good day?" I ask. "For your arthritis, I mean."

She takes a bite of her lobster roll, and then pats her mouth with a paper napkin. "Lots of pain and swelling in my knees, and sometimes a stiff back, too."

"What makes it happen?"

"It's a bit of a mystery," she says. "My body's signals get crossed, and my immune system attacks my joints, trying to fight an infection that isn't there. I take medications that calm things down, but the flares still happen every few weeks. They're more likely if I overdo things or if I'm stressed or under the weather, but sometimes there's no explanation."

"That sounds awful," I say.

She nods. "I used to insist it wasn't that bad and I could power through. But powering through often makes the pain worse, and the truth is, it's a pretty crummy deal, especially when it holds me back from doing what I want. I feel a lot better when I acknowledge that."

"If it's mentionable it's more manageable?" I ask. "Like you said when I first got here."

She smiles. "Exactly. Just like Mr. Rogers taught me."

The beach is filling up now. A bunch more families and couples come claim their spots.

"Now the big question is, how do you like that lobster roll?" Aunt Mary asks.

"I love it," I tell her, and she pumps a fist in victory.

"I was hoping you would."

I ask her if my mom used to like lobster rolls, and she pauses.

"Hmm. I don't think we ever ate lobster rolls as kids. I know she did *not* like regular lobster, which disappointed our father." Then she smiles again. "Her favorite dinner was tuna noodle casserole. Our mother used to make it with crushed-up potato chips on top. That might have been what your mom really liked, come to think of it. The chips. She'd 'help' our mom make it and eat half the bag."

I giggle. "She still loves potato chips. What else did she like when she was a kid? Other than surfing and black cherry ice cream?"

"Let's see." Aunt Mary finishes her lobster roll, then rolls up the paper wrapping and puts it inside her bag so it won't blow away. The air is getting chillier, so I zip up my fleece and slip the hood over my head.

"Well, she loved to read," Aunt Mary says. "And she was always telling stories about everything—her dolls, the seagulls, our neighbors. It's no surprise she became a writer." She laughs. "One summer, she and Danielle made their own neighborhood newspaper and tried to sell it door-to-door. The front page was an opinion piece your mom wrote about why Gray Island was the greatest place in the world. Our dad had a fit when he found out they were taking people's money. He made them give it all back."

I force another laugh, too, but it makes me sad that Mom used to love the island that much and now she doesn't. And the part about their dad having a fit doesn't sound very funny. I know Mom was never close with her father. He came to visit us for Thanksgiving a few times when I was a kid, but he never stayed long, and Mom was always relieved when he left.

The sky is mostly pink now, and the orange sun slips down toward the water. There's a family with two little girls in matching sweaters sitting on beach towels near us, and the parents hand each kid a juice box. The littler sister cries because she squeezes the box too hard and juice dribbles out, and the bigger one uses her own sweater sleeve to wipe the littler one's hands.

Sisters. Like Aunt Mary and Mom.

"Can I ask you something?" I say.

"Of course."

The beach is more crowded now, and the buzz of other people's conversations is louder than the crashing waves. A toddler who's maybe two or three laughs and happy-shrieks as he chases a seagull.

"What did you mean the day I got here when you said you'd pushed Mom to talk about things in the past?"

"Ah." Aunt Mary runs her fingertips over the fake-wood arm of her folding chair and looks out at the water. I figure she'll tell me to ask Mom or give me another baby gate analogy, but after a while, she says, "When we were kids, I always looked out for your mom. I was so much older, and she was this dreamy, imaginative kid who didn't always fit into our strict, practical family."

I nod because I want her to keep going, but it's hard to picture Mom as dreamy.

"That always felt like my role, to protect her, and I liked that. But once we were all grown up, I still worried about her and tried to protect her. And that wasn't what she wanted from me anymore."

I wait to see if she'll say anything else, and when she doesn't, I ask, "Was there an actual fight?"

She tilts her head to one side and back. "There were a couple of specific conflicts. Moments when my intentions were good, but emotions were running too high. I should have backed off."

My heart is beating fast now. It feels like I'm close to some kind of answer I didn't actually believe I'd get.

"What were the conflicts about?" I ask softly.

I'm afraid she won't tell me. I'm afraid she *will*.

She sighs. "I want to be open with you, Bea. But I also need to respect what your mom would want. I don't want to put my foot in my mouth and say things I shouldn't."

And I feel the same way I do when I'm up at bat and I earn a walk by laying off a pitch I'm pretty sure I could have driven. Regretful but relieved, too.

Around us, people gasp and *ahh* and cheer, and Aunt Mary points out toward the horizon. The sun's a fiery orange arch below the last strip of clouds, slowly flattening. Lower, lower, lower.

Gone.

It took so long getting ready to set, and we saw the exact moment it disappeared.

Everyone on the beach is quiet. This beautiful thing brought us all together, no matter what we were talking about a minute ago or where we're going when we leave the beach. It reminds me of the best parts of being on a team—the way everything else can fade away when you're all focused on one thing, together.

Aunt Mary reaches over to squeeze my hand, and I squeeze hers back.

"Thank you for bringing me here," I tell her. "It really did help."

She smiles. "I'm so glad. You're a good kid, Bea. You're a good kid, and you're doing the best you can during a hard time."

A *good* kid, not the *best* kid.

My shoulders relax away from my ears because I like the way that sounds. It fits—like a cozy, worn sweatshirt that's not too baggy but not too tight. I think it's different to *do* my best than to *be* the best. And I think I *am* doing my best, even if my best isn't always as good as I want it to be.

Eventually, kids start running around the beach again. People start talking and laughing and folding up their blankets and chairs.

We pack up our things and I take a selfie of the two of us—Aunt Mary and me, with the sky glowing behind our heads. I send it to Jessi and to my parents, too.

When we get back to the house, I ask if we can do another directed drawing before bed. We find a video for learning how to draw a sunset, and we follow all the instructions, drawing the lines of the horizon and then using crayons to make strips of red, pink, orange, and yellow. I'm tempted to use different colors from what the YouTube teacher says, so I could make my picture look more like the beach did tonight. I consider leaving out the palm trees, even though they're cute, since there aren't any palm trees here on Gray Island, or maybe adding in folding chairs and people.

But I'll probably mess up if I try any of those things. If I follow each step, one thing at a time, I know I'll make something pretty. So for now, that's what I do.

CHAPTER 14

The next morning, Nia and I get dropped off at camp at the same time.

She's bounced around positions during fielding drills the past couple of days. Sometimes she's still at short, but more often she's at second or third base, and she even took some fly balls in the outfield yesterday.

"Hey, listen," I say as we walk out to the field, but then I get stuck.

I don't want to tell her I'm sorry she's not getting time at shortstop because of me, because I don't regret being here and playing my best. But the coaches are announcing camp teams today, and Nia would be the starting shortstop for one of the teams if I hadn't switched to this camp, and now she probably won't.

"I know you've been playing other positions, not just shortstop, and—"

"Oh, don't worry about it," she says.

"You're not upset?"

She shakes her head. "Look. If you came to a basketball camp and showed me up at point guard, that would be a different story. But it's fine. What I really want is to make varsity basketball *and* softball as a freshman because my brother only made one varsity team. Coach Conway says my best shot at making varsity is being able to play a bunch of positions, anyway."

"Well, I can barely make a free throw, so you don't ever have to worry about me competing with you for point guard," I say, and she laughs.

We join Emery, Izzy, and a few other people on the sideline, and I notice Hannah isn't here yet, which is strange because she's usually early. I kind of feel like I *need* her to be here, because I don't trust that I'll be able to play my best if she's not.

She still hasn't arrived when Rose leads us into a classroom inside the closest school building, where the desks are pushed against the walls and chairs are set up in a circle.

"This is our mindfulness morning!" she announces. "As I'm sure you all know, the mental and emotional aspects of softball are just as important as the physical ones, so that's what we'll focus on today. We're going to start with a short mindfulness meditation."

I resist the urge to groan. My homeroom teacher used to make us meditate for stress relief last year, and I always felt like I was doing it wrong.

"I know it's a beautiful day and you want to be outside playing. But I'm telling you, this works," Rose goes on. "There are all sorts of studies that show meditating for at least twelve minutes a day improves your happiness levels, your sleep, *and* your performance on the field. It helps you stay in the moment and focus, and softball's all about focus, right?"

Well, if Rose thinks it can help make me a better softball player, I'm in.

I do exactly what she tells us. I sit with my feet flat on the ground, my butt toward the front of my chair, and my spine stacked up straight. I close my eyes and try as hard as I can to pay attention to my breath coming in through my nostrils and landing near my heart.

"Thoughts are going to come into your mind," Rose says. "That's normal. That's what our brains do—they think. You can name your thoughts if that helps you. Tell yourself, *that's a thought*. Or, *oh, there's a worry*. But let them pass by, like leaves floating through the air, or clouds gliding by in the sky. Or pitches outside the strike zone. You see them, but you let them go."

That's a whole lot easier said than done, though.

After a while, my brain says, *Whatever you do, don't think about the championship game,* and then it's too late. I'm *there*—letting the ball bounce out of my glove, throwing it over April's head, standing there frozen while Jessi marches over and grabs the ball out of my hand.

I tell myself those thoughts are balls outside the strike zone or leaves spinning in the breeze or fluffy white clouds way up in a pale blue sky, but none of that works. None of those images are powerful enough to chase the bad ones away.

There's a gentle hand on my shoulder, and I open my eyes to see Rose, standing right over me.

"If your mind is really wandering, you can try counting. Start at one. Count up to ten and then back down to one, and then start again. That's one way you can slow down your mind if you need to." She says it in her same meditation-leader voice, as if she's talking to everyone in the room, but I think she means me, mostly.

It must be obvious, how terrible I am at meditating. How I'm completely freaking out. What if she thinks I'm cutting corners again somehow? Not trying hard enough to do what she wants?

I count up to ten and back down to one, and thank freaking goodness, it helps. The numbers make those memories go hazy, and my heart slows down.

Finally, Rose eases us out of the meditation. "I want you to take three deep breaths. The deepest breaths you've taken all day. Breathe in love and appreciation for yourself, and breathe out love and appreciation for everyone else in the room. Because you're here, putting in the work to improve your game."

I don't know how to breathe love or whatever, but that's okay because I've done it. I made it through the meditation, and now we'll go back outside where we can talk and move and play, and hopefully Hannah will get here so I won't lose my edge.

But now there's another person in the room: a petite woman wearing a dressy coral blouse. Rose tells her we're all hers, and she introduces herself as Dr. Elena Alvarez, a sports psychologist who works with athletes of all ages who struggle with sports anxiety. She says to adjust our seats so we can see the SMART board at the front of the room, and then she clicks a button on a remote. The screen lights up with a slide that says, "Sports Anxiety and the Young Athlete: How to Break the Negative Cycle and Play Your Best," and I just—I *can't*.

She clicks the remote again, and now there's a picture

of a crying softball player with tears smudging her eye black. She's in the middle of a diagram that's labeled "Negative Thought Cycle." The word "nerves" is at the top of a circle, with an arrow that points to the word "error," and then another arrow that points to "pressure" and then "self-doubt" and then back to "nerves."

"Nerves aren't necessarily a bad thing," Dr. Alvarez says. "They can enhance your concentration and motivation. But they can also cause you to lose focus and make a mistake. Sometimes, that experience of feeling nervous and making a mistake can send an athlete into a self-defeating cycle."

Around me, people are nodding and "mm-hmming," calm as anything, but my heart is racing and my cheeks are way too hot. I can't seem to remember how to swallow. Dr. Alvarez tells us to turn and talk to somebody next to us about a time we've been in a cycle like this or seen somebody else go through it, and Emery turns to me with a freaking *smile* on her face, as if this is some kind of enjoyable activity. But there is no way I'm doing this.

"I need to go to the bathroom," I blurt, scrambling out of my chair.

Rose stops me at the door. "You all right?"

"Yeah! I'm fine! But I need to use the bathroom. Like, now. Is that okay?"

She watches me for a little too long. I want so much to please her, but I can't do what Dr. Alvarez is asking. I can't stay in this room.

"I *really* don't feel well," I say, and finally, she nods.

"Go. Of course. That way." She points down to the end of the hall and I bolt.

Safe inside the bathroom, I splash cold water on my face. My skin still feels hot, but my heart is slowing down.

*I'm okay*, I tell my reflection. *Everything is okay.*

I'm trying to figure out how long I can get away with staying in here when the door swings open and Hannah walks in.

"Oh! Hey," I say. "It's mindfulness morning. Do you know where everyone is?"

Her eyes are red, and I think she's been crying. "Hi. Yeah. Coach Flores told me."

She uses one of the stalls and flushes. I'm still standing at the mirror when she comes back out to wash her hands.

"You didn't have to wait for me," she says.

I shrug. "Everything all right?"

"Yep," she replies, but she won't look at me in the mirror. She turns off the water and scoots past me to dry her hands.

"I talked to Nia, just so you know," I say. "She says it's fine with her, playing other positions. Because that'll help her make varsity."

I'm thinking that might help Hannah like me a little better. That now she might realize I'm not some outsider who's swooping in and stealing playing time from people who deserve it. But when she finally meets my eye, she looks annoyed. Like she can't believe how clueless I am.

"That works out nicely for you," she says.

"Well, and for you," I point out. "You'll get your playing time at short, like you wanted."

"Sure, Bea," she says.

Then she walks out into the hallway, letting the door close in my face and leaving me wondering what the heck I said wrong.

By the time I get back into the classroom, the sharing part is over, and Dr. Alvarez is talking. I take my seat and tune out to avoid another freak-out. I count up to ten and down to one like Rose suggested—even though she suggested doing that if your mind accidentally wanders, not when you *want* your mind to wander. When I get bored of counting, I list all the players on the U.S. national team and all the players on the Yankees and all the things that make me a better shortstop than Hannah. And then, finally, we go back outside.

The coaches lead us through a few fielding and hitting exercises before lunch, and Rose pulls me aside after everybody else takes off.

"It seemed like that was pretty intense for you this morning, huh? With the meditation and Dr. Alvarez's talk."

I shake my head hard. "I just had a stomach thing. I'm fine now. I really am serious about camp and committed to doing every activity and all. I just felt sick."

Rose spins her long braid around one finger. "I know you're serious, Bea. Just don't forget about having fun, okay? And I hope you'll give the mindfulness meditation another shot when you're ready. I can point you toward some resources you might find helpful."

"That sounds great. Thanks so much!" I tell her.

But the truth is, nothing sounds great about that much quiet. The only thing that really sounds great is getting on that field for our scrimmage this afternoon and playing my heart out.

We get our official camp teams after lunch. Rose reads off the lists and explains she'll be bouncing back and forth, coaching everybody while Coach Conway takes charge of the Seagulls and Coach Flores leads the Sandpipers. I'm on the Seagulls with Emery, Izzy, and Nia, and Hannah's a Sandpiper. We lock eyes across the circle, and she gives me that same look from when she told me her position at the playground. There's a challenge in her expression, and I am going to rise to it because that's who I am. That's what I do.

Coach Conway wins rock paper scissors, so we're the home team, in the field first.

It's a scrimmage, not a real game. But we all put on our new team shirts—green for the Seagulls and yellow for the Sandpipers—and that giddy game-day rush zips through my arms and legs as I take my spot at shortstop.

Tasha comes to the plate to lead off for the Sandpipers and I smack my fist into my glove and call, "No outs, play's to first!"

I want her to hit me the ball. I definitely, definitely want her to hit me the ball.

This girl Kaitlin is pitching for our team, and Tasha gets into position to slap bunt. She sets up toward the back of the left side of the batter's box, angled toward first base so her momentum will already be taking her the way she wants to go.

"Yes, Tash!" someone shouts. "You've got this!"

"Come on, Kaitlin!" Emery yells from first base.

Kaitlin winds up, and her first pitch is low and inside, jamming Tasha, who fouls it off. Strike one. The next pitch gets more of the plate, and Tasha smacks it down the third base line and takes off.

Riley's playing third, and she charges the ball and fields it well, but Tasha's so fast that she reaches first easily.

"That's all right, Seagulls!" I say. "No outs, play's to first or second."

The next batter grounds out to Melanie at second base, but we don't have a chance at doubling up Tasha, so Melanie throws to first and Tasha advances. One out.

The third batter hits it hard but right at me, and I make the catch, no problem. And that means Hannah's up with two outs and a runner in scoring position.

*Hit the ball to me*, I will her.

Kaitlin's first pitch is over the outside corner. Hannah doesn't swing, and behind the plate, Rose calls, "Strike!"

The second pitch is inside, and Hannah fouls it off.

Two strikes, two outs.

The next pitch is shoulder high. It's the kind of pitch that's too high to hit well, but it looks so tempting that you have to remind yourself to lay off. Hannah swings hard and misses big, and that's that. Three strikes. Inning over.

"Yeah, Kaitlin!" Emery screams. "Way to make her chase it!"

"Way to go, Kaitlin. Good inning, Seagulls!" I call.

But I'm watching Hannah, who hangs her head as she walks off the field. I remember how she was late this morning, how her red eyes made me think she'd been crying. And how she said she needs this camp.

But that can't be my problem. *You can only control you*, I remind myself. I need to focus on *my* game, not hers.

I jog off the field, grab my bat and helmet, and go to the on-deck circle, where I take a few practice swings.

Our center fielder, Jasmine, leads off and lines out to third, so I'm up.

The first pitch is a strike, but it's too hard and low for me to drive. I lay off and wait for the second. This one's high and inside. I duck to avoid getting hit, and the count's even: one ball and one strike.

The third pitch is on the inside half of the plate. I swing and connect, rocketing a hit over Hannah's head. The left fielder gets to it fast, so I stay at first, and two batters later, Emery drives me in with a double.

The other Seagulls line up to high-five me and I soak this in: the cheers, the way it feels to be part of a team and know I came through.

I try not to wonder what Hannah's muttering to herself about as she kicks the infield dirt.

As the scrimmage goes on, I help Izzy practice her swing and scream my lungs out when she gets a hit. I give Nia tips on applying a tag when there's not a force out at third base. Emery and I come up with a "*caw-caw*" chant, since that's the sound seagulls make, and our whole team *caws* as loud as we can when we're batting.

I get one more hit and walk once, and I make a ton of plays in the field. Mostly routine ones, but one over-the-shoulder catch on an in-between pop-up and one super long throw from deep in the pocket behind third base that robs the other team's catcher of an extra-base hit.

Going into the last inning, the game is close. We're up 4–3, and the Sandpipers have the heart of their batting order coming up—their second, third, and fourth hitters.

Kaitlin gets the first hitter to line out to Emery. One down. The next batter smashes a line drive down the third base line, but Nia makes a diving catch. That's two hard-hit balls in a row, and we're lucky they were outs. Kaitlin's tired, and our luck could run out now with Hannah coming up to bat.

Hannah's settled in a little throughout the game, but she isn't quite herself. She hasn't technically made any errors, but she held on to the ball one time when a good throw could have gotten the runner out, and she's only gotten one soft hit.

She has a chance to do something big now, though.

"All right, Seagulls!" I shout. "Let's finish this right here. Two outs, play's to first."

"*Caw-caw!*" Emery adds.

But Kaitlin's first pitch is right down the middle, and Hannah crushes it into left-center field. Nobody's catching this ball. It might be a home run. It could definitely tie the game.

Our center fielder, Jasmine, chases it down. I run out toward her, getting into position to cut off her throw. I sneak a quick look in, and Hannah's motoring, already rounding second.

Jasmine finally reaches the ball, and her throw's strong and on target, reaching me on one hop.

Coach Flores is holding up her arms, yelling for Hannah to stop at third, but Hannah doesn't listen. She touches third base and keeps on running.

I catch the ball and rotate, firing the ball home with every ounce of strength I have.

My throw is perfect, right on target. Our catcher, Paige, snatches it out of the air and blocks the plate like a champ. Hannah slides, but Paige applies the tag.

"Out!" Coach Rose yells.

*Yes!*

"That throw was *sick*!" Kaitlin shouts. "And that tag. You're a beast, Paige."

We all run toward home plate to celebrate with Paige, but I'm watching Hannah, who's walking off the field with Rose.

Rose is scolding her the way she scolded me after sprints yesterday, but this is worse because everyone knows what Hannah did wrong. I can't make out everything Rose says, but I hear the words "respect your coaches."

*Respect your coaches.*

Hannah didn't listen to Coach Flores just like I didn't listen to Coach Yang when I threw to second on that dribbler in the semifinals. My risk paid off that day, and Hannah's didn't pay off today. But neither one of us was being disrespectful. Were we?

Dad would say you have to trust your gut no matter what. That any coach would rather have a player who runs through the third base coach's stop sign or makes a risky throw, because you can't be great if you don't believe in yourself. That if you have good instincts and don't second-guess them, the risks you take will pay off most of the time.

But is that right? Maybe every coach *wouldn't* rather have a player who ignores instructions some of the time. Maybe some coaches think you're being cocky or disrespectful if you listen to your gut instead of them.

I think of what Monique's mom said on Instagram. That she's tired of privileged white men like Dad thinking rules don't apply to them.

Dad *does* follow rules. Usually. And he cares about people and justice and the planet. But he didn't set up that account he was supposed to and he spent money that wasn't his. And . . . there *was* that time he drove Jessi and me to see a college softball game at Princeton for one of our surprise adventures. The game had been rescheduled so there was nothing to see, and he talked a grounds crew guy into letting us throw the ball around on the field so our trip wouldn't be for nothing, even though the guy said that wasn't allowed. And when I was having pain in my legs that turned out to be shin splints and the orthopedist's office didn't have any openings for two weeks, he called everyone he knew in the medical field until somebody pulled strings and got us an appointment the next day.

He did those things for *me*, and that was nice . . . but was it fair? Does he sometimes think our family deserves special treatment? Does he sometimes think he knows better than other people—that he's above the rules?

Do *I* think those things, too?

I'm all turned around inside my head as I walk through the line to say good game to the Sandpipers and then huddle up with the rest of the Seagulls to listen to Coach Conway give a post-scrimmage speech.

When he calls my name after everybody starts to walk away, I figure he noticed I was distracted. I'm about to promise I'll focus better next time. But what he says is, "You're one heck of a shortstop, Bea Bartlett. You've got a lot of heart and a lot of talent. Not to mention a cannon for an arm."

A cannon. Like Xander said, in another lifetime.

"Thanks, Coach."

"I saw the way you gave your teammates pointers and made sure everyone was having fun. I appreciate that leadership. I'm just putting this out there," he says. "Our star shortstop is a senior this year. I know you have some ties to the island, and we have some athletic scholarships available. It's something we can discuss, if you're interested. Just keep it in mind."

Wait . . . what?

Athletic scholarships. As in, what Rose had, and what Hannah specifically said she wanted. Does he not remember Hannah saying that?

"Wow. Thank you."

I could never *actually* leave my parents and go to boarding school here, though. I'm about to tell him that, but then he adds, "It would be a real pleasure to coach you. You remind me a lot of another outstanding shortstop I had the honor of coaching."

And I'm no longer capable of stringing words together because: *Rose.* I remind him of Rose.

As I grab my stuff and walk to Aunt Mary's car, my first thought is that I need to tell Jessi that Rose Marvin's high school coach just said I remind him of her. Except Jessi still doesn't know what I'm really doing here.

I need to tell her. As soon as I get back to Aunt Mary's house. As soon as I've filled Mom and Dad in on the scrimmage, I will.

CHAPTER 16

I'm hungry when we get back to Aunt Mary's house, so I grab a granola bar. But before I have time to finish eating it, my phone rings with a FaceTime from Dad. I take one more bite, wash it down with a swig of lemonade, and pick up.

My parents are there on the screen, their faces smooshed together. Dad's face is clean-shaven and he's wearing a light blue dress shirt, which makes him look more like his old self than he has in a while.

"Bumble!" Dad says, at the same time Mom says, "Hi, honey!"

And I don't *want* to feel the rush of annoyance that tightens my jaw. It's just . . . I *said* I'd call as soon as I got home. They couldn't wait two more minutes for me to eat something?

I push away the annoyance because they love me. They miss me. This is the longest I've ever been away.

"How was the scrimmage? Tell us everything!" Dad says.

So I give them the highlights and ask what's new there.

"Well, the house looks great," Mom says. "More people are coming to see it this weekend, and Rina's taking us to look at a few places across town. And Dad had a good meeting today."

She nods at him, signaling it's his turn to talk, but he doesn't say anything.

"Henry," she urges.

Finally, Dad says, "You remember Pete Calhoun? He worked with me at Damon Berger?"

"Uh huh."

He was a young lawyer at Dad's old firm. At the firm barbecue one year, he told Mom and me how nice Dad was to him—how patient Dad was when he messed up a memo for a client he was helping out with, and how Dad always made sure he got enough billable hours.

"Well, Pete's at a firm in Mertonville now—he moved after the merger, and he's got a big project he needs some help with. Research mostly, and drafting some briefs. It's a type of law I know well, so he thought of me."

"Wait . . . you're working for Pete Calhoun?"

Dad sighs. "I'm not exactly working *for* Pete. He's delegating work he doesn't have time to do."

I need to be supportive—I know I do. But I'm thinking of what Gran said a year and a half ago, that Dad was taking a risk by opening his own practice instead of looking for a job at another firm. Dad told her he was overqualified for the other positions he'd found and he'd worked at a firm long enough—he'd earned the right to work for himself. Except now here he is, taking pity assignments from Pete Calhoun, who used to report to *him*.

And anyway, I thought he couldn't practice law. Unless . . . I grab onto a glimmer of hope.

"Did the suspension get shortened or something, if you're doing lawyer work?"

Dad's face crumples, and I hate myself.

"No, honey," he says. "This isn't technically practicing law. A good paralegal could do it." His voice is so sad and quiet. All the energy's been sapped right out of it, because of *me*.

"It's nice that it uses your knowledge and skills, though. You'll do a much better job than any paralegal could," Mom cuts in.

She has a smile glued on her face. She's building Dad up because I shot him down.

I force myself to sound happy. To be Dad's Beatrix and bring him joy. "Yeah, that's great! Pete Calhoun is lucky to have you."

It isn't very convincing, but I don't know what to add. There's a too-long silence I have no clue how to fill.

"Well, we shouldn't keep you on a Friday afternoon after a big win," Mom says. "Have fun with Aunt Mary tonight. We love you so much."

*We shouldn't keep you.*

That's what she says to other grown-ups when she's done with a conversation and wants to get back to what she was doing before: *I shouldn't keep you* or *I'll let you go*. It's a more polite way of saying, "I don't want *you* to keep *me* for any longer," which is what she really means.

She wants me to get off the phone because I'm not doing my job. I'm supposed to make Dad happy, and I'm not.

"Okay. I love you, too. Have a good night. Bye," I squeak, hitting the button to end the call.

I stare at the blank screen. Half of me thinks I should call back right away and try again, but the terrible truth is that the other half of me is relieved to have hung up. Relieved to be far away. Dad is hurting, and I don't *want* to call back. I'm mad that he took that risk, opening his own practice, and then let everything turn into such a mess. I want *space*.

For just a second, I think about that scholarship Coach Conway mentioned. It's a fantasy—I know it is. But how great would it be to go to school here on the island, where the ocean is never more than a couple of miles away and I can just be *Bea*, not my parents' Beatrix? Where there aren't any Bartlett Benches in the center of town and no one knows how Dad got in trouble or how I fell apart.

My phone dings with a text from Emery, saying she and Izzy just got ice cream in town and they're going to her house for pizza and then to watch a movie on the beach.

*Wanna come? If you give me the address my dad says we can pick you up.*

I don't want to stay here thinking about Dad and Pete Calhoun for one more second, so I bolt downstairs to ask Aunt Mary if I can go. She says it's fine with her, and pretty soon I'm in the back seat of Emery's dad's car. She and Izzy brought me a melty soft serve from Timeless Treats, and it feels disloyal to Danielle to eat it, but it's not like it would make things better for the Creamery if I don't.

I promise myself I'll invite Emery and Izzy to get ice cream at the Creamery next week and convince them how much better it is, and then I dig in.

And it's only after I eat the last cold, sweet bite and answer Mr. Lau's questions about where I'm from and whether I've been to the island before that I realize: I promised myself I'd call Jessi and I still haven't.

But there's nothing I can do about that now. I breathe in the fresh, slightly salty air that streams in through the open sunroof, making my hair dance. For now, at least, I'm in this beautiful place with these nice new friends who bought me ice cream. Jessi's probably having fun with all our friends at home. I might as well have fun here, too.

Later, when we get to the beach where the movie is, we buy popcorn from a little stand and find a good place to set up our folding chairs to watch.

There are a lot of people here already, and we spot Nia, who's wearing a green-and-yellow Gray Island Academy basketball sweatshirt. She's sitting on a blanket with a boy who looks a lot like her. She waves, so we leave our chairs and go say hi.

"This is my brother Calvin," she tells us. "Cal, these are my friends from camp. Bea, Emery, and Izzy."

"I know you," he says, pointing at me.

I'm confused, because I don't think I've ever seen him before, but then he adds, "I was lifting at the gym at school today and I caught the end of the game. I saw you gun down that girl at the plate."

He lets out a whistle, and I feel myself blush, but Nia rolls her eyes.

"Stop looking for excuses to tell people you lift weights, Cal. No one's impressed."

He flexes his sort of scrawny biceps and grins. "Oh, come on. Your softball friends seem a little impressed."

"My softball friends could lift more than you," Nia counters, and Calvin laughs.

"Possibly true," he says.

Izzy sets her popcorn down in the sand to zip her jacket, and a seagull hops over and pecks at it.

"Ew, stop!" she says, picking up the bucket so fast that popcorn kernels go flying. The seagull helps itself to a piece and scurries away.

"It must sense a connection to you, Izzy," I joke. "Since you're a Seagull, too."

Izzy shoos away two more seagulls, and Emery starts the *caw-caw* chant. It doesn't discourage the birds from helping themselves to the spilled popcorn, but it does make Izzy, Nia, and me crack up.

"I feel like I'm missing something," Calvin says, and for some reason that makes us laugh even harder.

Right now, that depressing conversation I had with my parents feels like it happened to somebody else. Like I could set it down in a room, close the door, and walk far, far away. I think again about how great it would be if I could go to school here instead of having to go back to Butler. I could hang out with Nia. We could see Emery and Izzy if they ever came to their island houses on school breaks. I could do directed drawings with Aunt Mary and watch beach sunsets all the time.

Emery and Izzy squeal and run off to hug another one of their summer friends, and then Nia's parents walk over holding popcorn and sodas. Her mom is petite and white with straight, brown hair, and her dad is tall and Black with a shaved head.

"Mom, Dad, this is Bea," Nia tells them, "from my camp. Mary Westover's niece, remember?"

Nia's dad shakes my hand and tells me they love Aunt Mary, and Nia's mom's face lights up. "Bea! How nice to meet you. Is your mom here, too?"

She glances around, searching, but I shake my head.

"Well, tell her Trish Malone said hi, will you?"

"Of course," I say.

And then she takes a step closer. "I was so glad to hear your mom got remarried, Bea," she says more quietly.

"I'm so glad she has you, after everything. She deserves all good things."

Nia's eyes bug out and she mouths a sorry, and Calvin puts up a hand to shield himself from the awkwardness, but it's fine. I've had a whole lot of conversations just like this one back in New Jersey. With people who knew Dad and Allison, not Mom and Evan. About *Dad* deserving to be happy and have a loving family and all that. But still—same idea.

"Thanks," I tell Nia's mom.

"My sister," she says. "She's had some of the same mental health struggles Evan did. She's in a good place now, mostly. But it's been a long, hard journey, and there are still tough times."

I'm nodding along, accepting her sympathy the way I do when people gush about how sad it was to lose Allison, and then I freeze.

Mental health struggles? *What?*

"I've thought of Evan so many times. And your mom, too. That kind of loss . . . devastating."

But Evan died of *cancer*. That's what Mom told me.

She told me he was sick for a long, long time, and he got better and then worse. She said it was cancer. Didn't she?

"Mom." Nia grabs her mom's arm. "You don't just *say* things like that."

"Well, we *should* say things like that. We need to end the stigma. There's no shame in discussing any of this."

"Sure," Nia says. "But maybe not with someone you just met who might not want to talk about it right this second."

A voice comes over a speaker saying the movie will begin in five minutes.

"It's okay," I say. "My seat's over there, so I'd better . . . It was nice to meet you all. See you Monday, Nia. Bye!"

I give a little wave and walk through the thick, soft sand over to where Emery and Izzy are already sitting in their chairs.

I'm numb, and at the same time every part of me is aching.

Did Evan not have cancer? Did Mom lie?

Was it suicide?

The movie starts, and I sit there with my eyes locked on the screen, but I don't process a single thing that happens.

I thought I sort of understood the kind of loss Mom had gone through, even if she wouldn't ever go into detail. But maybe I don't get it at all. Maybe I don't get *her* at all.

# CHAPTER 17

After the beach movie finally ends, Emery's dad drops me off back at Aunt Mary's.

Aunt Mary's sitting on the living room couch reading a book, with a bubbly, yellow-gold beer in a tall glass on the coffee table.

"Hey, how was the movie?"

"Did Evan not actually die of cancer?" I ask.

Her smile falls and her eyebrows edge in together.

"Did . . . what?"

"Evan. That's what Mom told me, that he died of cancer."

At least I think she did.

We talked about it in fourth grade. That April, Danielle called on Evan's birthday to see how Mom was doing, and Mom had the phone on speaker while she was making the brownies in his honor. She didn't know I'd come downstairs. She was crying, and she said something about how life kept passing by so fast and she wasn't sure if she was doing enough to keep his memory alive. She said she still had dreams about the day he died.

Then she saw me and told me to go upstairs and watch an extra episode of *Liv and Maddie*, and I rushed back up because it was scary, seeing her that upset. And then I realized that I didn't actually know how Evan had died. I only knew that Allison's death had been sudden, and Evan's hadn't.

Jessi's grandmother had been sick for a long time with cancer, so that night at bedtime, I asked if Evan had been sick with cancer, and Mom said yes. I'm sure she did. She definitely didn't say no. But now I can't remember the details of the conversation.

"Did someone say something about Evan tonight?" Aunt Mary asks.

Which pretty much confirms it wasn't cancer. If it had been, she would have said so.

"Trish Malone?" I say. "She said all this stuff about mental health issues and her sister having them too and how there shouldn't be a stigma. Did Evan . . . was he depressed or something? Did he . . ."

I trail off, and Aunt Mary stands and walks over to me, but then she stops, like she doesn't know whether to hug me or pat me on the shoulder or what. Finally, she rests her hand on the outside of my arm. "That must have been really confusing."

"What was it, if it wasn't cancer? What actually happened?"

Aunt Mary hesitates. "I'm so sorry you're getting hit with so many things at once."

"Can you please just tell me how he died?" I practically scream.

She shakes her head. "I'm so sorry. I think you need to talk to your mom."

Right.

Because now's a *perfect* time to call Mom out on lying and demand the truth, which she probably wouldn't even give me, anyway.

"Fine, don't tell me! Just keep secrets from me like everybody else!"

The words burn my throat because I know Aunt Mary doesn't deserve them. I know this isn't her fault, but I can't calm myself down.

I bolt upstairs to the room where I'm staying and take out my phone. I'll figure it out myself.

I know the year Evan died and two of the places he lived—Gray Island and Boston. But I don't know his last name. How do I not even know his last name?

I search for an obituary, a cause of death, *something*, but I can't find him. None of the links that come up seem right. But then I add Mom's full name, and *there*.

There's a short, vague obituary that tells me his last name—Frazier.

I say that out loud. *Frazier. Evan Frazier.*

There's a picture, too—a different one than the photo in Mom and Dad's room, but I recognize his thin face, dark hair, and small smile. But the obituary doesn't tell me how he died. I go back to the search results, and then I find an essay with Mom's byline in *Boston Globe Magazine* from 2005. "When New Love Brings Old Fears."

That . . . does not sound like the kind of piece Mom would ever write. She writes for parenting magazines all the time, but she won't share specific details about Dad or me. That's one of her rules—to respect our family's privacy and never publish anything too personal.

My heart jumps to my throat as I click the link and start to read.

The essay is about how Evan was depressed for years. How much he suffered, and how hard he fought, and how, finally, he took his life. That's how Mom put it. He took his life. That verb, *took*. It's such a nothing word. People take an umbrella when it rains. They take a day off if they have a cold. But . . . poor Evan. Poor Mom.

And anyone who read this essay in 2005 knew what really happened. Everyone on Gray Island knows. But I had no idea.

The next part is about how Mom and Dad reconnected a year later in an online grief forum for people who had lost a romantic partner. And—*oh*. How Mom's sister didn't think the relationship was a good idea. That's what the essay says. That Aunt Mary thought Mom should be with someone steady and well-adjusted. Someone who wasn't also in the depths of grief, because they might pull each other down deeper. And Mom thought that was wrong until she looked for a Q-tip in Dad's medicine cabinet and found his prescription for one of the same antidepressants Evan had been taking before he died.

My heart drops from my throat to the bottom of my stomach, smooshed between kidneys and a liver and whatever else is down there.

Dad was depressed after Allison died.

Evan was depressed, and then he died.

I think of Dad's pale, stubbly face. The way he was just sitting there staring at his blank laptop screen on the last day of school. The way he put his head in his hands at the kitchen table because I couldn't make myself sound okay about having to move. The way I begged him to send me to sleepaway camp even when he hesitated, and the way his face crumpled this afternoon when I made him feel even worse about doing work for Pete Calhoun.

There's more in the essay. Stuff about how Mom's old fears flooded back and threatened to pull her under, but she wouldn't let them. She chose love and hope and Dad. I think it's supposed to be a happy, empowering ending.

But I'm stuck on the part in the middle.

What if Dad's depressed again now? What if I've made him *more* depressed? What if . . . the next thought that flashes inside my brain is too terrifying to let myself think at all.

I need Dad to be okay. I need our family to be okay.

A text comes in from Jessi, but I can't talk to her right now. I dismiss the message without even reading the words and throw my phone onto the carpet.

What's *wrong* with me? I should have stayed in New Jersey with my parents and been their Beatrix, but instead I ran away to Gray Island. Just tonight, I was fantasizing about staying here and going to Gray Island Academy and abandoning Dad when he *needs* me.

Who cares if Dad isn't perfect? Who cares if he's done things wrong? He's my dad and we're a team and I will do anything to help him be okay.

I dive onto the bed and bury my face in the pillow. My tears soak the pillowcase, and I wish I were on my own bed in my own room in New Jersey.

I want to go home. I need to go home.

CHAPTER

18

I wake up the next morning on top of the comforter, still wearing my jeans and sweatshirt from last night. It takes a minute before everything comes back: what Nia's mom said. What I read in Mom's essay.

My stomach grumbles and my heart aches.

I need to apologize for snapping at Aunt Mary, and I need to eat something. And then I need to figure out how to get myself home to Dad.

I head downstairs to the kitchen, where Aunt Mary is sitting at the table with a mug of coffee and an empty plate, reading.

"Hey there," she greets me, closing her book. "I got muffins at the farmers market. Strawberries, too. Help yourself." She points to a paper bag and a dish of small, bright red berries on the counter.

I make myself a plate and sit down next to her.

"How are you holding up?" she asks at the same time I say, "I'm really sorry I yelled at you."

She pats my hand. "I get it, Bea. This is a lot, kiddo. What I want to know is how you're doing this morning."

I shrug. "I know what happened now, mostly. I found an obituary online. And an essay Mom wrote about Evan and Dad and . . ."

I trail off, not sure whether or not she knows what Mom wrote, but I can tell from the way her lips press together that she does.

"Ah," she says. "The essay."

"That was the fight that drove you apart, right? Or one of them. What Mom wrote about in the essay, about you not liking Dad."

She shakes her head. "Bea. No. The conversation we had before she wrote that essay—yes, that drove us apart. And the essay did, too. I was hurt that she took the things I'd said out of concern for her and used them to make a point. To support this thesis that felt too simple for real life."

*To control the message.* That's the phrase that pops into my head. Like she wanted to do with that written statement for Dad.

"But I want you to know that I've *never* disliked your dad," Aunt Mary says. "I was worried about your mom jumping into taking care of someone who was just as wounded as she was. I thought she needed help. And time. But I always thought your dad was a really good guy."

I take a bite of sweet, fluffy blueberry muffin. The outside is crunchy, and the inside is flaky and soft. It seems sort of impossible that it can be both those things in one bite, but it is.

I take a deep breath and ask, "What do you think now?"

She looks puzzled for a second, and then she realizes what I'm asking. Does she still think Dad's a really good guy? That's what I want to know. *Can* he still be a really good guy after what he did? Is it possible to be both those things at once—a really good guy *and* a person who messed up so badly he can't be a lawyer anymore?

"Oh, Bea," she says, her voice scratchy. "Your dad loves you, and he loves your mom, so much. And maybe what matters most is what he does *next*, to make things right."

She stands and pulls me up to stand, too, so she can hug me for real. It feels good, leaning into her. Her arms are soft and steady, and the hug is tight enough that I know she means it but not so tight that I feel stuck.

I'm glad I've been here with her, so glad. But now I need to go. I sit back down, and she sits, too, and then I tell her. "I think I have to go home. Like, as soon as possible."

Her eyebrows shoot up, and she folds her hands on the table and taps her thumbs together. "Wow. Well, I'd hate to see you go so soon. But if you feel like you need to be home with your parents to process all this, then I get it."

I'm relieved she's not objecting, but that isn't what I mean. "I just . . . they need me," I tell her, and she tilts her head to one side and then the other, as if she has to jostle my words into place inside her brain before they'll make sense.

"You think they need you?"

"Yes. Because . . . that essay. Dad was depressed before. That's what Mom wrote. He was taking medication and everything. He might be depressed again."

She nods slowly. "That's possible."

She says it so calmly. Why is she being so calm?

"They need me to help them!" I say. "To bring them joy!"

My voice is too loud and I don't want to yell at her again, but she doesn't know how our family works. She doesn't understand.

"You do bring them joy," she says. "Of course you do, always. But you don't have to be there with them to make them happy. I think the best thing you can do for them—and for yourself—is what makes *you* happiest right now, whether that's staying or going home."

The best thing I can do for them is what makes me happiest.

I can tell if a ball is hit well by the sound it makes when it connects with the bat, and I can tell these words are true by the way they feel when they echo through my body.

"You're right," I say.

I can make my parents happiest by staying here for one more week and being happy myself. They'd be worried if I came home early. Dad would feel even guiltier. I should stay here and show them they don't need to worry about me. Show them how okay I am.

*Show* them.

What if I really *could*? What if I could get Mom and Dad to come here next weekend, in time for the camp championship game on Friday? They could see how well I'm playing now.

Coming to the island might be what Mom needs to help her take down those baby gates she's put up, and Dad could escape to this place where people still think he's a really good guy. It could be a throwback to that summer he spent here, when he had all those admirers after the Slow Pitch Social and . . . wait a minute.

The Creamery is struggling and needs a boost. Mom

and Dad need something happy and special. I was on the Field Day committee at school. I know how to plan a big event.

"What if we could bring back the Slow Pitch Social?" I ask.

Aunt Mary blinks. "The Slow Pitch Social? For next summer, you mean?"

"I was thinking next weekend. And I could convince my parents to come."

Her eyes go wide.

"I know it sounds like a long shot," I admit. "It's super last-minute, so it couldn't be anything fancy. But I could get the other people at camp to come and bring their friends or parents or whoever, and that would be plenty of people to make two softball teams. And the Creamery could sell tons of ice cream and everyone would remember how it's a zillion times better than Timeless Treats."

"That's quite a vision you have there," Aunt Mary says.

Maybe she thinks it's silly of me to believe I could make something like this happen.

Gran sometimes tells my parents that the trouble with treating me like I hung the moon is that I'll think I can accomplish anything and be disappointed when I can't, but one time Mom told her, "Or maybe she'll think she can accomplish anything and so she *will*."

"It could be at that park with the handball court even," I say. "I know there's not a real field, but we could just set up bases in the grass. Or maybe the Academy fields would be free."

Coach Conway was putting up signs after camp yesterday for a baseball clinic somebody's running there this weekend. Maybe he'd let us use one of the fields next weekend if no one else is.

"It's a really lovely idea," Aunt Mary says. "But the fields at the Academy would probably cost a lot of money to rent out. It's a pretty fancy place."

I hadn't thought of that, but I shrug.

"It can't hurt to ask, right?" I say, and she nods.

"I suppose not. But, Bea. Even if you could somehow pull this off—you know it wouldn't fix everything hard your parents are dealing with."

"I know," I tell her.

But my gut is telling me that it would be a pretty excellent start.

Coach Conway's email address is on all our camp materials, so I send him an email explaining my idea and ask if there's any way we could use one of the fields. Then I shower, get dressed, and FaceTime Dad.

It's just him today. He says Mom's upstairs working in the office—trying to finish an article before Rina the Realtor takes them to look at houses on the other side of town.

"How are you doing?" I try to say it extra seriously so he'll know I'm asking about more than just how his morning's going, but he just says he's fine and that he and Mom went for a nice walk early this morning, before the day got too hot.

"So listen, I was thinking," I start.

"Uh oh, sounds dangerous," he says, and I grin—not because it's actually funny, but because it's such a *Dad* thing to say. If he's making corny jokes like that, he must be okay-*ish,* if not all the way okay.

"I'd really, really like it if you and Mom could come here next weekend. The camp championship's Friday morning, and I want you to be there. I want you to see me play and stay for the weekend."

He blinks. "Oh!"

He doesn't say anything else, so I add, "I know Mom's probably going to say things are too busy with the house. I know it's hard for her, coming here. But it would mean a lot to me. I think it would mean a lot to Aunt Mary, too."

"Oh, Bumble." His voice is shaky, so he clears his throat and tries again. "If you want us there, of course I'll come."

*Of course.* Because he's Dad, and he'll do anything for me, no matter what.

"What about Mom?" I ask, and he hesitates.

"I'll talk to her."

But *I* should talk to her. If anyone can convince her, it's me.

I ask Dad to take the phone upstairs. She says, "Henry, I need an hour, *please*," when he knocks on the door, but her voice softens once she hears I've called.

"Bea," she says, taking the phone. "What's going on, honey? Are you all right?"

It's the first time I've seen her face since I found out the truth about Evan, and some of that panic from last night rushes back, but I hold it off.

"Yes. I'm okay," I say. "But I want you and Dad to come to the island to see me play in the camp championship game on Friday and to spend the weekend here with Aunt Mary and me. I think it would be really good. For all of us."

"Oh, Bea," she says, already shaking her head.

"*Please.* I know things are busy. I know it'll be hard. But I need you to come."

Dad says something that I can't make out, and Mom sighs.

"It's important to me, Mom. Please."

"Okay," she says finally. "We'll look into ferry times. We'll make it work."

"Thank you," I tell her. "It's going to be great. It's going to be just what we need."

I cross all my fingers that I'm right about that, and a few minutes after we hang up, I get an email back from Coach Conway. He remembers the old Slow Pitch Socials, and he loves my idea. He says the softball fields are available, and there's a whole initiative at Gray Island Academy to build community with the rest of the island. As long as I'm working with Gray Island residents and businesses to make it happen, then the event fits right in with their program. We just need to follow some basic rules for disposing of trash and taking care of the fields—which *does* include replacing divots, Aunt Mary will be amused to see—and we can have them for no charge. He'll be there to help make sure everything runs smoothly, too.

I rush back out to the porch, where Aunt Mary's reading.

"My parents are coming!" I tell her. "And we can have the Academy fields for free. Look!"

I show her Coach Conway's email on my phone, and she lets out a whistle. "You are a force to be reckoned with, Bea Bartlett. That's terrific. Let me know how I can help."

But I don't know yet how she can help, because I don't

actually know how I'm going to pull any of this off. I need a plan.

I take a piece of the paper Aunt Mary and I use for drawing and make a list. I can find out from Coach Conway about supplies—folding tables for food, water jugs, a first aid kit. I can invite everybody at camp and tell them to invite more people, too. Maybe I'll make flyers to hang up around town. I'll call it the Spur-of-the-Moment Slow Pitch Social, so everybody will understand it's kind of last-minute and low-key. And if I'm going to work with "Gray Island residents and businesses" like Coach Conway says, then the Creamery seems like the best place to start.

# CHAPTER 19

Thirty minutes later, I lock up Aunt Mary's old bike outside the Creamery.

I have a text from Dad, saying he and Mom booked ferry tickets for Friday morning, so they'll spend the night at a motel on Cape Cod Thursday night and be here in time for the camp championship. I reply with a bunch of hearts and confetti, and then I peek inside the front windows of the Creamery, which won't officially open for another twenty minutes.

Everything was quiet before it opened last Saturday, when Aunt Mary and I came for pre-lunch ice cream. But today, a bunch of people in maroon Creamery T-shirts are rushing around inside, moving tables and blowing up balloons.

Danielle notices me and jogs over to open the door.

"Hey there, Bea. What's up?"

Before I can answer, a man comes out of the back to tell her they're down to the last two gallons of cookies 'n' cream in the deep freezer. And then a teenager at the register calls, "Danielle, the credit card reader's off-line again!"

Danielle shakes her head. "I'm sorry, Bea. We're doing a birthday party at twelve thirty, which we don't usually say yes to during prime customer time, but . . ." she trails off and glances up at the clock on the wall. "What's going on?"

I tell myself that if she's desperate enough to do a birthday party during prime customer time, she'll be excited about the chance to sell lots of ice cream next weekend even though right now she's super busy. I explain as quickly as I can, and her eyes light up when I say my parents are coming.

But then a bright pink balloon pops, and somebody screeches.

"It's a really nice plan, Bea. We'd love to sell some ice cream. I can send someone over with a few gallons and some toppings and cones, and I'll do my best to be there for part of it, too, okay?"

I thank her, but I need more help than that from a Gray Island resident to make this event happen. I could probably ask Nia . . . but if Mom and Danielle were working together planning the Slow Pitch Social all those years ago, it feels like Hannah's the right person to help me now.

"Is Hannah around?" I ask.

Danielle points toward a door in the back. "She's upstairs. You can go on up."

She rushes over to the cash register, and I take one of my walking-up-to-the-plate psych-up breaths before heading to the back of the store and up the stairs.

I knock on the door at the top, and Hannah yells, "Coming!"

I thought there might be a Creamery office or lounge or something up here, but when Hannah opens the door, I see that it's an apartment. This must be where she and Danielle live.

She raises her eyebrows. "Please tell me you're not here to apologize for throwing me out at the plate yesterday."

I wince. "No way. I just . . . I have a question for you."

"Okay," she says, leaning against the doorframe.

The kitchen is behind her, and there's a box of generic brand Cheerios out on the counter. I can see photos on the refrigerator, too. One of Hannah and Danielle, back when Hannah still wore glasses and had really long hair. One of a big group of people, all wearing those maroon Creamery T-shirts. One of tiny Hannah with a missing front tooth and a giant pink-and-white polka-dotted bow in her hair.

Maybe it's better that Mom and Dad have cleared out some of our personal stuff for the house showings. It's a little too intimate, looking inside the home of somebody you really don't know.

"Bea. What's your question?"

"Have you heard of the Slow Pitch Social?" I ask.

She shakes her head.

I tell her as much as I know, considering I've never been to one. "And it's how my parents met a long time ago. They're coming this weekend, and the fields at the Academy are free. So I'm trying to make it happen again, but I need help." I pause. "Do you want to help?"

Her eyes narrow. "Hold up. What? Why?"

"Why am I asking you to help? Because I need somebody who's from here. Who knows people and can help me invite local businesses and stuff."

"And why are you doing this?" she asks.

"Oh. Because my parents have always told me about it. I think it sounds really fun." I leave out the part about how they *need* something really fun. "And my aunt Mary says the Creamery used to sell a ton of ice cream. And Coach Conway was into the idea of doing a community thing."

Now she raises her eyebrows.

"It would be a pretty good way to show him you're

community-minded and a leader and all, in addition to being a good softball player. If you're still hoping to convince him you deserve a scholarship."

She's quiet for a second, and then she nods. "I'm better than good, though. For the record."

"Okay."

"I *am*," she says, and I smile.

"I don't disagree."

"You'll email Coach Conway and tell him I'm doing it with you?" she asks. "Make me sound all impressive and leader-y?"

"Leader-y?"

She rolls her eyes. "You can use your own words. You know what I mean."

"I'll use a bunch of those buzzwords from that mission statement he read us."

"Good. I have to go to the Cape to see my dad tomorrow, though. So I can't help then. But I'm free now."

She steps to the side so I can enter the kitchen and then leads me into a living room with a small couch, two armchairs, and tall bookcases.

I show Hannah my planning list, and we divide up some of the tasks. I'll ask Coach Conway about folding tables and other supplies when I email him about her helping, and I'll see if Aunt Mary can put us in touch with anyone who used to help plan the event in the old days. Hannah's in charge of social media, which she already does for the Creamery. She'll make graphics for us and create an event on the Creamery's Facebook page. She thinks we should make flyers to hand out and post around town, too, so she goes into her room to get paper, markers, and pens.

"Here. We can each make one, and then we'll make copies on my mom's printer."

I try to remember the steps from that directed drawing video to make a softball player on mine, but some of my shapes are lopsided and the whole thing's a mess. Hannah writes out the information with fancy, perfectly even letters and draws in a softball, bat, glove, and ice cream cone like it's nothing.

"Okay, mine's embarrassing," I say. "Let's just use yours."

"I'm sure yours is fine," she says, but then she looks. "Oh wow, yeah that's terrible."

"Rude!" I throw a marker cap at her, but she manages to catch it.

"Please, respect the equipment," she says, echoing what Coach Conway said when Emery was chasing Izzy around trying to squirt her with a water bottle, and Izzy tripped over a base and knocked it out of position.

I crack up, and she picks up my terrible attempt at a flyer. "Maybe I should just recycle this."

"I think that's best for everyone," I agree.

She makes a bunch of copies of her flyer, and we swing back through the Creamery, where a whole lot of seven-year-olds with sugar highs are making a whole lot of noise, to tell Danielle where we're going.

We hit the bagel place first and leave a flyer with the two high school kids working behind the counter, who say they'll give it to their boss. Next, we go to the bakery.

The woman behind the counter looks about our parents' age, and she rushes around the counter to give Hannah a hug.

She asks Hannah a bunch of questions, one right after the other: about softball camp and how the Creamery's doing and when Hannah's going to her dad's.

Hannah keeps glancing over at me while she answers in as few words as possible. Camp's good. The Creamery's fine. She's going to her dad's tomorrow.

"Two weekends in a row?" the woman asks, and Hannah nods.

"That was the deal. To make up for the weekends I

missed in the spring for softball games. I was supposed to go yesterday but everything got mixed up, so." She shrugs. "Tomorrow. Anyway. This is Bea. She and I are planning a Slow Pitch Social for next weekend."

The woman, who introduces herself to me as Meg, takes a flyer and says the bakery would be delighted to participate. "For you, Hannahbear, I'll even donate one of my cookie decorating kits if you're doing a raffle like they used to. I could make it softball-themed."

"That's so nice." Hannah looks at me. "A raffle sounds good?"

"Definitely," I agree.

We make a note of Meg's donation, and then Hannah gets her to pose with an enormous M&M cookie for a picture we can use as a teaser on social media.

"Where to next, Hannahbear?" I ask when we leave, and Hannah groans.

"If you want my help, you will never say that again."

"Okay, okay!" I laugh.

We go to the deli next, where Larry, the man behind the counter, promises to send an employee to sell an assortment of hoagies and says he'll donate a gourmet gift basket for the raffle. He poses with a big jar of his special, secret-recipe pickles for Hannah's teaser picture.

"You should say, 'Does this PICKLE your fancy? Then come to the Slow Pitch Social!' Get it? Pickle, tickle. That's good, right? I'll let you have that one for free."

"That's something all right," Hannah says, and we thank him and keep going down the street.

Hannah knows people at every single place we go. Her old babysitter, Ramona, is the manager at the pizza place. A girl named Elisa, who's a barista at the coffee shop, used to ride the school bus with her.

When we leave the coffee shop, she stops to talk to a blond girl with a North Shore Sands swimming T-shirt and a boy with longish, light brown hair. They're sitting at an outside table drinking lemonade and sharing a cupcake, and she introduces them to me as Annabelle and Jeremy.

They have a summer internship at a science institute on the other end of the island, where marine biologists are researching the coral in the ocean just off the coast here, and Hannah wants to know all about what they're doing there.

"The institute is so cool," Hannah tells me after we say goodbye and walk away. "Did you know the coral in the ocean here can survive extreme temperatures?"

I shake my head.

"The water gets super cold, but the coral's okay. If sci-entists can figure out how it survives, that could help save coral reefs in other places where they're dying because of climate change. We took a field trip there for school. I want to get an internship next summer once I'm old enough, if I can. You have to be fourteen." Her eyes are extra bright and her voice is, too.

"Wow. That's amazing." I've spent so much time figuring out all of Hannah's strengths and weaknesses on the softball field, but I didn't know anything about *her* before today, and I like the Hannah I'm getting to know. A lot.

"It would be, yeah. If we even still live here next summer."

And just like that, all the brightness from a second ago is gone.

"I didn't know you might be moving."

"Well, if the Creamery goes out of business, we'll have to."

That must be why she wants a softball scholarship to the Academy so much. Because then, even if she and Danielle move somewhere else, she could basically stay.

"Probably to Cleveland, if my dad gets his way." She spits out the word "Cleveland" as if it's poison and hustles across the street. "Anyway, we've gone enough places, right? We have the Creamery, the bakery, the deli, the coffee shop, and the pizza place, and maybe the Bagelry. You think that's enough people to sell food?"

I scramble to catch up. "Yeah, I think so. But wait. Your mom would move to Cleveland, too? Even though your parents aren't together?"

Hannah says hi to a lady standing in front of a souvenir shop and then sighs. "I don't know. My dad's from Cleveland, and his family's there. He wants to move back, but he also wants me to visit every other weekend. Mom says we won't leave the island if we can help it, but anything's on the table if we do."

"Oh. Wow."

She nods. "I mean, I know he loves me and that's why he wants me nearby. But wherever I live, sometimes I'm going to have a weekend game I don't want to miss, or a friend's party or whatever. And if I choose the game or party and it's a Dad weekend, it's a whole thing."

I think of Emilia, whose Dad moved to Pittsburgh after her parents split up. It's too far to go for just a weekend, so she and her brother go weeks without seeing him, but then they stay with him for at least a week at a time on school breaks. She once told me the first day with him is extra hard, and so is the first day back with her mom. *Dad-lag*, she calls it—like jet lag, except it's not a time change they're adjusting to, it's everything. I thought that sounded hard, but Hannah's way does, too.

"Tasha's mom's a therapist, and Tasha says it's super

codependent that he makes me feel guilty if I have something else going on." She looks at me expectantly, like she's waiting for me to weigh in.

"Oh. Um, I don't know what that means."

She shrugs. "It's, like, when a parent has an unhealthy attachment to their kid and makes the kid feel responsible for their emotions. I don't think that's really it, though."

We reach the Creamery and she sits down on a bench right outside. I hesitate for a second before sitting down next to her.

"Seems like the situation sucks, either way," I say, and she nods.

"I had a huge fight with him yesterday morning." She's still holding a small stack of flyers, and she folds the corner of the top one over, unfolds it, and folds it again. "That's why I was late to camp. He wanted to take me out to dinner at this nice restaurant to celebrate the end of seventh grade, but he could only get super early reservations. I would have had to leave before the scrimmage was done and take the two o'clock ferry, so I said no, and he said he was trying to do something special. It was bad."

She rips that triangular corner piece all the way off, then balls it up between her fingertips.

"I know he was trying to make me happy. But it wouldn't have made me happy to leave camp early, you know?"

I *do* know, kind of. My dad would never schedule any-thing that made me miss softball. But I know the sinking feeling I get if Dad tries to do something that'll make me happy and it doesn't. Like when he bought me a dress for the holiday concert at school last year from a store Jessi and I used to love when we were, like, nine. I wore it so he wouldn't feel bad, but it was long and babyish and green, and all the other girls' dresses were short and black. He noticed how different it was from what my friends were wearing, and the look on his face when he asked if I would have preferred something else still cracks my heart in half.

"I get it. Yeah," I say.

"You're lucky your parents care about sports, though. My mom once told me your dad's your biggest softball fan. And he takes you to the batting cages and to watch college games and never misses seeing you play."

"Oh!" I want to ask what else Danielle has said about Dad, but it isn't the right time for that, so I clear my throat and say, "Um. He does, yeah."

She straightens the stack of flyers, making all the edges match up except the one she tore off.

"My dad doesn't care about softball at all."

That gives me an idea. "Could you invite him to the camp championship on Friday? Because if he hasn't seen you play in a while and he sees how good you are and how much you love it, then maybe he'd understand better. That you care about him *and* softball."

She looks down at her feet and crunches up her toes so they don't reach the end of her sandals, then straightens them. "Nah. He wouldn't come."

"Why?" I ask.

"Because he'd have to take the day off work. And he says Gray Island's my mom's turf. He didn't come to any of my games all season. He's not going to come for this."

"You could try?" I suggest. "Tell him it's important to you? That's what I told my parents."

"You don't get it, Bea. Not everybody's parents can drop everything and come see them play in a softball game that doesn't even count."

Her voice comes out sharp, and I flinch. "You're right. I don't know your dad. I'm lucky my parents can come."

She sighs. "I shouldn't have said it like that. I just . . . when my mom thought maybe we could stay at your house last fall, she told me all about how nice your dad is. How happy it made her when your parents got married because your mom deserved someone wonderful after everything she'd been through."

My heart swells because it feels *so good* to hear someone call Dad wonderful.

"She told me all these nice things your mom had said about you, too, because she thought you and I would be friends if we visited. She made you sound like this perfect girl with a perfect life. And then you showed up at the last second for camp, and you refused to throw with me at the park but then acted like you owned the whole infield. And Coach Conway obviously loves you, and . . ." She trails off and shakes her head. "I don't know. I'm sure your life isn't perfect. I'm sure you have your own stuff."

She's waiting for me to say something.

She confided in me, and she's waiting for me to confide in her, too, but . . . I can't. Not when my parents are coming in less than a week and I need Gray Island to be a place where everyone still thinks Dad is wonderful.

"Sure," I finally say. "Everybody has their stuff."

But I don't tell her any of mine.

"Okay," she says, standing up. "Well, I should go back in. I promised my mom I'd help this afternoon. Don't forget to email Coach Conway. I'll do some posts when I'm done working behind the counter."

"Sounds good. And Hannah? Thank you for doing this with me. This was fun. I'm excited."

"Yeah," she says, smiling a little. "Me too."

She goes back inside the Creamery, and I unlock the bike from the rack out front.

And today *was* fun, and I *am* excited. But as I ride back toward Aunt Mary's, I have that same feeling I get when the batter right before me makes the last out in a game, so I don't get to come to the plate. Like when I shut down that conversation with Hannah, I missed a chance at something that might have been really good.

CHAPTER

20

At camp on Monday, Coach Conway compliments Hannah and me on our "impressive initiative and leadership," and Hannah tells me she invited her dad to come on Friday after all and he really might come.

"That's awesome," I say. "I'm so glad."

"Me too," she says. "I told him we're going to crush the other team, so it'll be a good opportunity to see me win."

I laugh and tell her we'll see about that, and then she catches up with her friends and I catch up with mine.

Later, the coaches explain that we'll be doing a bunch of Seagulls versus Sandpipers challenges this week, and Coach Flores teaches us how to play a game called 3, 2, 1, Run. She sends Melanie to second base and has the rest of us Seagulls line up behind third while the Sandpipers line up at home plate. Then she sets three balls on the ground, spaced out down the third base line. When she says "Go," the first person on my team has to sprint to pick up the first ball and throw it to second base and then pick up the next one and the next, throwing each ball to second while the first Sandpiper sprints to second from home plate. If the first Seagull player throws all three balls to Melanie and she catches them cleanly and steps on the base before the first Sandpiper makes it to second, we get a point. If any of the balls drop or the runner gets there first, the Sandpipers get a point. Then the first Seagull to throw trades places with Melanie at second and Melanie goes to the back of the line to wait for her turn to throw.

Emery pushes me to the front of the line. "You have the best arm," she whispers. "You should go first."

Coach Flores blows her whistle before I'm really ready, but I take off, picking up the balls one by one and firing each one to second. My third throw hits Melanie's glove and beats Tasha to the base by two steps.

The whole game is loud and silly and fast. Once everybody on my team has gone, we switch—Sandpipers in the field and Seagulls running. Then we switch back, and I'm at the front of the line again.

Coach Flores blows her whistle, and I hear all my teammates cheering as I sprint down the line and throw the first ball right at Melanie. I pick up the second ball and wind up to throw again, but I let go all wrong. The ball sails over Melanie's head with everybody watching. I hear groans and someone yells "no" but I keep going, picking up the next ball and throwing that one too, right on target.

The other team gets a point, but as I run to second base, the only thing I feel is relieved. Because I'm okay.

I didn't freak out after one bad throw, even though everybody was watching. I brushed off my error and made the next play.

And all day long, I don't tell myself to beat Hannah a single time. I don't keep track of which of us does better in each drill. I just focus on myself, and I have *fun*.

"Good job today, Bea," Rose tells me at the end of the day, and even though I didn't do anything all that spectacular from a softball perspective, I grin.

"Thanks, Coach Rose," I reply.

A couple of hours later, my phone rings when I'm getting out of the shower. It's Jessi. I'm sort of in a rush, since Aunt Mary and I are going to a beach barbecue with some of her friends, and talking to Jessi isn't likely to be quick.

I've been so caught up in plans for the Slow Pitch Social that I still haven't called her. I haven't even responded to the "what are you up to?" message she sent Friday night, when I was so upset about Mom's essay. I feel more distant from Jessi than I ever have—even when her family went to Japan for a whole month last summer. And it's my fault, since I keep blowing her off.

I dismiss the call but send a text.

*I'm about to go to a barbecue. Everything okay?*

She writes right back. *Yeah. Can you call me after though?*

My stomach twists, because that's kind of ominous.

*Sure. Is something wrong?*

*No. It's about Xander. Everything's fine but I want to give you a heads-up about something.*

I gnaw on the inside of my cheek. I don't want a heads-up about Xander. If he said something about me, if he likes someone else, if he's officially *with* someone else already, even. Whatever it is, I don't want to know. Not when I have less than a week left here on Gray Island. I'll deal with Xander and everything else once I'm back in New Jersey. I don't want to ruin my time here obsessing about it now.

*Could you maybe tell me when I get home actually? I kind of need a break from Xander stuff.*

I add a smiley face in case that sounds harsh otherwise, and she takes a long time to reply.

When she finally does, all she says is: *OK.*

The next day is a bad pain day for Aunt Mary. She limps down the stairs and eats her breakfast in the living room instead of the kitchen so she can prop up her swollen legs, and she takes heavy-duty anti-inflammatories that make her arthritis pain better but hurt her head and stomach. She insists she can drive me to camp since it isn't far, but then she asks Danielle to pick me up at the end of the day so she can rest.

"I want to feel a hundred percent by Friday when your parents come," she tells me. "So I'm taking extra good care of myself now."

She says both Linda and her friend Aruni are happy to help with food and errands during a flare, but she's done so many nice things for me since I've been here. I want to do nice things for her, too. I ride her old bike into town for more milk and paper towels when we run out, make tortellini for dinner, and do the dishes, and I keep her company in the living room, watching TV.

Between helping Aunt Mary, planning for the Slow Pitch Social, and camp, the next couple of days are too busy to think too much about that last text exchange with Jessi or wonder what she was going to say about Xander.

And then it's Thursday, the day before my parents arrive.

Hannah has a doctor's appointment right after camp, but we're meeting at the Creamery afterward to hand out one more batch of flyers and collect the rest of the raffle donations for the Social on Saturday.

I ride Aunt Mary's bike into town and see that Danielle's car isn't back in its reserved spot yet. So I buy my usual black cherry and try it in a waffle cup instead of a cone this time. I sit on the bench outside to eat it while I watch for their car, and I'm almost finished when I hear my name.

"Bea! Hey!" It's a boy's voice. A *familiar* boy's voice.

I nearly drop the ice cream cup when I see him across the street.

No. I shade my eyes from the afternoon sun in case the light's playing tricks on me, because I cannot be looking at the person I think I'm looking at. But it's him.

It's Xander, here on Gray Island, wearing a red Butler baseball shirt and waving as he jogs toward me. *That's* what Jessi wanted to tell me.

"Bea!" He's *right* in front of me. Two feet away, tops. "Jessi told me you were here."

That one tuft of hair is sticking up just like always, and my body reacts the same way it has every time I've seen him since March. Too-fast heart. Too-hot skin. Too-wobbly stomach. All down my arms, I have that static-electricity feeling I get when I wear tights with a dress in the winter.

"I was gonna tell you I was coming, but I texted you and you didn't reply so I wasn't sure . . ." He trails off and stuffs his hands in his pockets. The gesture is so familiar that I squeeze my container of ice cream too hard and what's left of the waffle cup cracks.

"You literally just wrote *hey*," I point out.

He ducks his head a little. "Yeah."

"Xander. What are you doing here?"

He sits down on the bench slowly, glancing over to give me a chance to object, I guess, but I'm too surprised to say anything.

"I'm on vacation. We usually rent the same house in Martha's Vineyard for two weeks in August, but my dad has a case that might go to trial then, so my mom found a place to rent here."

The ice cream is heavy in my gut as I scan the other side of the street to see if his dad's nearby, too.

"Oh." Xander watches me look and winces. "He's play-ing mini golf with my sister. I'm supposed to pick up the pizza we ordered, but then I saw you across the street. So, yeah. Now I'm here. With you. Hi."

His cheeks are pink, and he's babbling. That day after the semifinal game, I felt powerful when I realized he was nervous. But I don't feel powerful at all right now.

This is a really little bench, and he's sitting so close that our knees would be touching if I shifted my left leg over just an inch. He smells like sunscreen on top of his usual laundry-detergent scent, and I *miss* him somehow, even though he's literally right here.

I miss the excitement of spotting him at school each morning and noticing which shirt he was wearing. I miss all those things I used to imagine might happen: him sliding his hand over and lacing his fingers together with mine. Him asking me to slow dance at the eighth-grade semiformal next fall. Him leaning in and kissing me, tasting like those wintergreen mints he shared with me during study hall once.

"How are you?" he asks. "I mean, after everything."

*Everything.*

The word is huge and vague and suffocating. There's too much sympathy in his adorable face, and I realize: He's not nervous because he still likes me. He's nervous because he feels *bad* for me and he doesn't know what to say that will help.

The rest of my ice cream is melting now—halfway to soup. I set the cup on the arm of the bench and scoot toward it, giving myself as much space from him as I can.

"I'm doing *great*," I say.

"Oh! Well . . . good! I just wasn't sure, after the championships, and—"

"Yeah. That was sweet of you, but you don't have to worry. I'm great."

He nods, but I don't think he believes me.

"I'm here for a softball camp, actually, and it's been amazing," I go on. "What happened at the championships was a one-time thing."

"Good!" He lowers his voice. "And things with . . . the other stuff . . ."

*The other stuff.* He can't even say it.

"Things are fine," I say, because apparently *I* can't say it, either.

He puffs up his cheeks and lets the air out in a whoosh. "I really wish my dad hadn't written that stuff online. He gets so worked up about anything he thinks is hypocritical or unethical. I don't think it was personal against your dad."

He doesn't think it was *personal*? It felt pretty freaking personal to me.

And I mean, I wish his dad hadn't written that stuff, too. And I wish *my* dad hadn't screwed up. And I wish Xander had never worn that bright yellow shirt last spring so Tyson wouldn't have made fun of him and then maybe my crush never would have activated, and I wish I hadn't fallen apart at the championships. But all those things happened anyway, so what good is wishing for something else?

"Bea." Xander reaches his hand toward mine, just *exactly* the way I used to wish he would. Except I don't want this now. This isn't how it was supposed to go.

I pull my hand away, and he flinches.

"I'm sorry."

"You don't have to be sorry." My voice is too loud—I know it is—but I can't make it come out softer. "And you don't have to worry about me. I love it here on Gray Island. I might stay here, actually. We might move."

As I blurt out these words, I think maybe—just maybe—they could be true. If this weekend goes well—if Mom can handle being back and take her gates down—then maybe we *could* move here. Dad could practice law here once his suspension ends even if he can't at home, because no one on Gray Island would have a reason not to trust him. The Bartlett Benches wouldn't be there in the town square making him feel like a disappointment, and I could be a day student at the Academy like Nia, so I could still live in a house with my parents. We could still be a team.

Xander's eyebrows shoot up. "Wait . . . really? I heard

your house was on the market, but I didn't know you were leaving New Jersey."

I squeeze my hands into fists, focusing on the sting of my fingernails digging into flesh. I *hate* that he heard that. I don't want Xander to know that or anything else about me and my family.

"I basically got offered a softball scholarship to this boarding school here, and I'm thinking about accepting it," I blurt out.

His mouth drops open, and mine does, too.

Coach Conway didn't offer me anything official. He's the *high school* coach. He probably meant I could maybe get a scholarship for freshman year, not eighth grade. But I can't take the words back now.

The bell on the door to the Creamery jangles, and I look up just in time to see the door shut. If only I had stayed inside to eat my ice cream, then Xander wouldn't have spotted me. I wouldn't feel like I just took a line drive in the stomach. But that's another useless wish.

"Wow," Xander says. "I mean, I'd miss you if you didn't come back to New Jersey. But congratulations."

He notices the stack of flyers in my lap. "Slow Pitch Social?" he reads, and my heart plummets.

"Please don't come," I squeak. "I'm organizing it. Well, co-organizing it. My parents will be there, and I want it to be this whole perfect surprise for them, and I don't want anyone there to remind them of stuff at home. Just, *please*."

Two minutes ago, all I wanted was to wipe the sympathetic look off his face, and now I'm basically begging for his pity.

"Geez. Okay," he says quietly. "I won't come."

"Thank you," I reply, just as quiet. "I hope you have a good vacation. Maybe I'll see you back in New Jersey."

He stands up, and he's a little wobbly on his feet, as if he's stepping off a boat onto solid land. "Bye, Bea. Good luck with everything."

"Bye, Xander."

I watch him walk away, his head down and his hands stuffed in his shorts pockets. I throw my cup of too-melted ice cream at the trash can a few feet from the bench, and it bounces off the rim, sending ice cream soup dripping onto the ground. I try to mop it up with my napkins, and then I notice: Danielle's car is parked in her reserved spot, less than ten feet from where I was sitting.

She and Hannah must have gotten back while I was talking to Xander. They must have walked right past us on their way inside.

How much of that conversation did they hear?

# CHAPTER 21

I rush inside to find Hannah, but she isn't in the store. The teenager behind the counter tells me Hannah's upstairs, so I run right up and knock.

Hannah groans when she opens the door. "Go away, Bea. I have nothing to say to you."

That thing I blurted out about Gray Island Academy and the scholarship. That's what she must have heard.

"Hannah. I can explain," I insist.

Except . . . can I?

How can I explain why I was so desperate to make Xander stop pitying me without telling her what Dad did?

She sets her hands on her hips. "I'm listening."

"I . . . Xander is a guy I know from home. We liked each other. I think. But then everything got complicated."

"I don't care about your *boy* problems," she spits out. "You got me to help you plan the Social to convince Coach Conway I deserve a scholarship to the Academy when *you* wanted a scholarship all along? When you maybe even *had* one?"

I shake my head. "I didn't."

She raises her eyebrows. "Did Coach Conway offer you an athletic scholarship to Gray Island Academy or not?"

"No. Not exactly. He mentioned it was a possibility."

"And you kept that a secret and roped me into working my butt off for this random last-minute event that would benefit *you*?"

"And the Creamery and other local businesses!" I say.

She lets out a one-second laugh. "Like *that's* why you're doing it."

I start to contradict her, but she's right. I was mostly doing it for my parents. I was mostly doing it for me.

I try again to explain. "The thing about me maybe getting a scholarship—I was overwhelmed seeing Xander. I made it sound like a sure thing when it definitely isn't."

"I really don't care how *overwhelmed* you were." She pushes the door closed, but I stick out my foot to stop it.

"Wait. Please," I say, and she sighs.

"Look," she says. "I'm not bailing on the Slow Pitch Social when it's two days away and people are counting on it. I'll collect the raffle items myself. But I don't want to talk to you. So please just do *one* thing that isn't completely selfish and *go*."

I pull my foot away, and she slams the door. I stand frozen in front of it, staring at the gray-black scuffs on the white paint and the dull silver doorknob.

My phone rings, and it's Jessi. My heart speeds up. I really, *really* need to tell Jessi about going to camp here now that I just told Xander.

I rush down the stairs, push open the side door of the Creamery, and walk out into the sunny late afternoon. "Jess!" I say.

And what she says back is, "What the hell, Bea?"

Oh no.

"You talked to Xander," I say.

"He just called me. He actually does that—returns my texts and calls."

"I'm sorry, Jess. I shouldn't have . . . I should've—"

"Told me you're going to softball camp on Gray Island and not just there on vacation, and there's a chance you might move there for good? Yeah. I agree. You should've."

Her voice is so angry. I've never heard her sound this angry. I almost crash into a kid holding a Timeless

Treats ice cream cup, who tells me to watch where I'm going.

I apologize to the random kid, too, resisting the urge to shout that the Creamery's way better, and then I sit in a chair outside the mostly empty bagel place so I won't bump into anyone else.

"Jess," I start.

"Are you moving?" she asks.

"No. Well, yes. We need to sell our house. But we're not leaving New Jersey. One of the coaches here did say something about how maybe I could get a scholarship to the boarding school here, but that was kind of wishful thinking, what I said to Xander."

"Saying you're leaving New Jersey was wishful thinking?" she squeaks.

Her voice doesn't sound angry anymore. Now she sounds like she might cry—like she might be crying already, even. I press the palm of my hand into the metal tabletop.

"That came out wrong. The truth is I just . . . I needed a break. From Xander, like I told you the other day. But also, from *everything*."

"Everything including me," she says.

It's a statement, not a question, and as much as I hate to admit it, it's true.

"Kind of," I reply. "I needed to get away. I wanted to be in a new place where I didn't know anybody. Where nobody knew what happened with my dad or at the championships."

There's a long silence before she says, "You're not going to the sleepaway camp with us."

That's a statement, too.

"No," I admit. "I didn't know how to tell you. I didn't want you to pity me even more. I didn't want to let you down again, after that championship game."

She lets out a strangled laugh. "You thought you'd be letting me down less by keeping this a secret? Who am I going to room with now? Some random person? What if they're awful?"

"I'm sure they won't be awful. You get along with everyone! And you'll have Emilia and Monique," I point out.

"I wanted to go with *you*," she replies.

I press my hand into the table even harder and chew on the inside of my cheek. I'd almost convinced myself she wouldn't mind that much that I won't be there. That she'd be happy to have time with just Emilia and Monique—that she might need a break from me, too. But I can hear it in her voice, how much she minds.

"I'm so sorry," I tell her. I don't know what else to say.

I hear her brothers laughing and yelling in the background, and she sighs. "I'm supposed to be watching Jack and Justin. I have to go now. I'll talk to you later."

And that's it. She hangs up.

There are tiny red diamonds on the palm of my hand from the crisscross pattern on top of the table. The guy working at the bagel place comes out to tell me they're closing up and bringing the outdoor furniture inside, so I need to leave. I stumble back to where I left Aunt Mary's bike locked up outside the Creamery and think of that thing Gran says—how my parents think I hung the moon.

The thing about the moon is, it revolves around the earth. It can't float off and go where it wants. Our gravitational pull keeps it spinning and spinning, around and around.

Am I a person who thinks everything else revolves around me?

Am I selfish, like Hannah said? Is Dad selfish, to have taken the risk to start his own practice and been so careless with other people's money? Do we think the things *we* want are more important than what everyone else wants? Do we think we're somehow above other people's rules?

I put on the helmet Aunt Mary lent me, get onto the bike, and pedal hard. I have one of those cushiony training softballs in my bag, and that park with the handball court isn't too far away. I want to throw a ball, hard, so I go there instead of back to the house.

It's more crowded now than it was last time I was here. There are a bunch of little kids on the playground, and some older kids are playing basketball. One of them is Nia's brother, Calvin, and I rush past without saying hi, heading straight for the handball wall. I grip the ball in my right hand, rotate my torso, pull my arm back.

And then my brain says, *What if it happens again? What if you can't throw the ball? How terrible would that be, if you've hurt Jessi and Hannah and lied to Xander and the yips come back? If Mom and Dad come all this way only to see you self-destruct?*

My heart is hammering and my palms are sweaty as I stuff the ball back into my bag without even attempting a throw.

I get on the bike and wobble enough that I think I might tip over, but then I steady myself, and I'm off. I ride past Aunt Mary's and down the path to the private beach. I lock the bike up on the rack near the entrance and walk out onto the sand.

I pass kids making a sandcastle, grown-ups reading on towels under beach umbrellas, and seagulls scavenging for food. A napkin blows up into the air, spinning in the breeze.

It's a whole lot windier on the beach than it was in

town. My hair whips around my face, and a big gust sends a spray of sand flying. I put my sunglasses on to keep the sand out of my eyes and take off my sandals, holding them in one hand as I walk to the water's edge.

There really is something about the ocean.

The way it stretches out so much farther than I can see. The cold, bubbling waves that lap over my feet. Welcoming me, it feels like, despite everything I've done wrong today. I sync my breathing to the rhythm of the waves swishing in and out, and my heart and brain slow down a little.

*Okay.*

I need a dose of perspective, and then I'll know what to do next. I'll figure out a plan.

I walk away from the water and find a patch of sand where I'm as alone as I'm going to get. I sit down, shielding my face from sand as another gust of wind blows. Once it passes, I unzip my wallet and take out the folded-up photo of eighth-grade Allison.

I rub my thumb over the worn creases where it's been folded so many times and push up my sunglasses so I can see her shiny pearl earrings, her poufy bangs, her big smile. So I'll feel grateful and determined and ready to make things better.

*I'm here and she's not,* I remind myself.

I have a chance to make things right.

But there's a tightness behind my ribs that won't loosen. The perspective check isn't working.

Allison's photo is supposed to make me feel grateful and motivated. Ready to suck it up and make the most of things.

But Allison's gone, and Evan's gone. I'm worried Jessi's not my best friend anymore and I'm scared I'll self-destruct on the field again and I'm terrified that Dad isn't actually okay.

Another gust of wind blows through, spraying sand everywhere. I shield my eyes and blink away the gritty bits that rain onto my face . . . and I lose my grip on Allison's picture. It flies right out of my hand.

*No!*

I scramble up and run after it, but there are little kids in my way, hitting a small blue ball back and forth with wooden paddles. I loop around them, but the sand is so thick it's hard to move fast. The wind changes course, taking the picture way off into the dunes.

And then the wind stops, and the paper falls. I scramble along the edge of the dunes and stop in front of the place where I think it must be. I'm about to climb over the little fence to get it back when I see the sign.

*Please Keep Off Dunes! Dunes provide a home for birds and a barrier for storm surges. Just a few footsteps can destroy them.*

I need that photo. But I don't want to destroy the dunes.

I don't want to be a selfish jerk who thinks the world revolves around her.

The picture must be *right there*, but I can't reach it without breaking a rule that matters and causing harm.

I wait to see if the wind might pick up again and blow the picture back to me, but it doesn't.

I tell myself I can make another copy of Allison's picture as soon as I'm back at school, and I gather up my things and go back to the bike.

But as I pedal home to Aunt Mary's, I can't shake the feeling that I've lost something irreplaceable. Maybe more than one something.

## CHAPTER 22

Back at the house, an unfamiliar maroon car is parked at the end of the driveway, and Linda's on the deck with Aunt Mary.

I only met Linda a couple of times, when we had lunch in Manhattan with her and Aunt Mary during their adventure weekends, but I recognize her voice before I see her. She has a raspy, jolly voice—as if she's always on the verge of laughing.

I'm really not up for making small talk, and I want to pretend I don't notice them out there and go straight in the front door, but Aunt Mary calls me over.

"Hi there, Bea!" Linda says, standing up to hug me. "Nice to see you."

I glue on a smile. "Nice to see you, too."

"I hear you're quite the organizer, huh? Making this Slow Pitch Social happen out of nowhere and in record time!"

I'm used to being told I'm "quite the softball player" or "quite the student," but "quite the organizer" is new.

"Thank you," I say. "A lot of people have helped."

"But you had the vision, and you figured out how to break it down into actionable steps," Aunt Mary points out from her chair. "That's an impressive skill."

And . . . I guess that *is* a pretty good skill to have, now that I'm thinking about it. It's what those YouTube art teachers do—breaking a drawing down into pieces. And what Mom does when she takes on articles that require a ton of research, and what Dad did back when he taught me to swing a bat and throw.

Linda finishes her glass of iced tea and says, "Well, I'm looking forward to it. I've got to hit the road, but I'll see you both Saturday."

Aunt Mary starts to stand, but Linda tells her not to be silly and bends down to hug her. Just before Linda gets into her car, she calls, "Try the turmeric tea! And my acupuncturist!"

"I said I will!" Aunt Mary calls back. Then she shakes her head, smiling a little. "Linda has a lot of ideas about things that might help with the arthritis pain."

I can't tell if Aunt Mary is touched that Linda cares about helping or annoyed that Linda's being bossy about something Aunt Mary obviously knows more about. The whole thing is kind of mystifying to me, that they were together for years and now they're not, but they can just sit on the deck and drink iced tea together. Xander and I never even *kissed*, and it hurt to sit too close to him on a bench.

I wonder if *that's* a skill—being able to handle something really sad, like a breakup or a death or even just a crush that fizzles or some weirdness with your best friend, without putting up gates and shutting down.

"She also brought us dinner, which means a very big step up from pasta," Aunt Mary says. Then she puts a hand up to block the sun and squints as she looks at my face. "You look upset." She pats the chair next to her. "You want to sit and talk?"

I think about that thing she said my first day here—that anything you're feeling is mentionable, and when something's mentionable it becomes more manageable.

I take a big psych-up breath, and then I sit down in the cushioned wicker chair next to hers and tell her pretty much all of it—what I blurted out to Xander, why Hannah's so mad at me, all the things I kept from Jessi.

"Do you think I'm selfish?" I ask when I'm done, and she shakes her head.

"I think you're a good kid who's having a hard time and doing her best," she says, just like she told me the other day. "And I think the fact that you're asking that question, reflecting on what you feel bad about—that says a lot."

"But what if my best isn't good enough?"

"It is," she insists. "If it's your best, it has to be."

I pick at a piece of wicker that's come loose on the arm of my chair. "But I can't do my best at every single thing at the same time. I've been so focused on doing my best at softball and doing my best to plan the Slow Pitch Social and make my parents happy, but then I wasn't doing my best at being a friend."

"Oh, Bea." She reaches out to put her hand on top of mine. "Even when we do our best, we come up short. Everyone does. We all focus on one area and neglect another. There are only so many balls you can juggle. Some of them are going to drop every once in a while."

I picture myself attempting to juggle three, four, five softballs and missing one, then another—watching them hit the ground and roll far away.

"What do you do after they fall?" I ask.

Aunt Mary looks out across the street, where the wind makes her neighbors' chimes jingle. "I think you pick them up," she says after a while. "Maybe set a few down in a safe place while you deal with the others. And I think you give yourself some compassion. Especially when things are this difficult. You appreciate how hard you're trying."

I think about Aunt Mary appreciating her knees on days when she doesn't have pain, and Rose telling us all to breathe in love and appreciation for ourselves at the end of that meditation. I *try* to breathe in love and appreciation for myself right now, but then I remember how mad Hannah was and how sad Jessi sounded, and I'm too disappointed in myself to feel any love at all.

"Also, Bea." Aunt Mary shifts in her seat so she can look me right in the eye. "It isn't your job to make your parents happy. Their happiness isn't your responsibility. No one can be responsible for another person's happiness."

That word Hannah used comes back to me: "codependent." When one person is too dependent on another. When one person makes another person feel responsible for their emotions. But that word doesn't fit my parents and me. Of course we depend on each other.

People depend on other people to be happy and safe. That's how relationships work. I think Linda still depends on Aunt Mary to fix things around her house, and Aunt Mary depends on Linda to help with stuff if her pain gets too bad. Even playing softball means depending on your teammates to do what they're supposed to do when the ball comes to them.

"Do you hear what I'm saying?" Aunt Mary asks, and I nod because I do *hear* her. I'm just not sure she understands how my family works.

We eat Linda's delicious zucchini enchiladas, and when we're finished, Aunt Mary asks me if I'm up for doing more art. I'm assuming she'll turn on her laptop to find another video, and that sounds predictable and relaxing. But instead she takes out a bag of new supplies.

"I went to the art store to get what I need for my watercolor class next week," she says. "The teacher suggested playing around with the paints before the class starts. You up for trying that?"

She pulls out a large pad of thick, slightly bumpy white paper and a bunch of paints—some in tubes and some in a rectangular palette thing that looks like a fancy version of the Crayola kind I had as a kid.

Starting with nothing but paint and white paper reminds me too much of art class at school, where I can never make anything that resembles what I see in my head.

"I don't want to waste your nice paints," I say. "I think I might go to bed early actually. Try to get a good night's sleep before the camp championships tomorrow."

"You wouldn't be wasting anything," she tells me, but I go upstairs anyway.

I spend a while trying to decide if I should text Jessi or Hannah to apologize again, but I can't figure out what to say. So I get into bed, and then I just lie there for ages, nowhere close to sleep. I start worrying about how exhausted I'll be tomorrow for such an important day, and how much harder it will be to play well if I can barely stay awake, and that pretty much guarantees I'm way too worked up to drift off.

After a long time, I hear Aunt Mary make her way up to bed, and I go downstairs for a glass of water and a change of scenery.

There's a piece of Aunt Mary's fancy watercolor paper on the kitchen table, along with some of her paints and paintbrushes. She wrote me a note on a Post-it that says, "For Bea, in case you need a little art challenge tonight. I dare you to have <u>fun</u> and <u>play</u>." She underlined the words "fun" and "play" the same way she used to underline "always" when she'd write every year in my birthday card that I was always welcome to visit.

I don't have much to lose, so I fill a little dish with water and dip a paintbrush into it.

I have no plan at all when I swirl the brush into the blue paint. I just twirl and dot and stripe the paper. I use the blues, reds, yellows, greens, and pinks, letting the different shades bleed together. Some of the color combinations look nice. Some of them really don't. What I create isn't pretty or impressive, but no one knows or cares. Eventually, my eyelids get heavy and my limbs do, too.

I clean the brushes and set my strange creation on the desk in my room, under the cute, precise drawings on the bulletin board.

I get back into bed and somehow, finally, I manage to drift off to sleep.

CHAPTER
23

The next morning, Aunt Mary drops me off for the final half day of softball camp and tells me she'll come back soon with my parents to watch the game.

"You'll be great," she says. "Good luck out there. Or break a leg, swing a bat—whatever a person's supposed to say before a softball game."

I laugh. "Good luck works."

As I walk away from the car, I remind myself of the plan I made when I woke up this morning after way too little sleep. First, apologize to Hannah but don't freak out if she stays mad. I can only control what I say, not how she reacts. Second, focus on playing the way I know I can play.

Those are the only two steps for now. I'll worry about everything else later.

I find Hannah right away. She's standing next to the bleachers with a bunch of people surrounding her, and she's reading something out loud off her phone.

As I walk over, the other girls look at me and their eyes go wide.

"Hannah," Tasha says. "That's enough."

But Hannah keeps on reading from the screen of her phone, and it only takes a handful of words—*regrettably, responsibility, poor judgment*—for me to recognize what she has.

It's the statement my parents wrote with help from Public Relations Lynn and shared on Dad's website. Hannah's reading it in a loud, sarcastic voice.

Hannah knows what happened.

All these girls know what happened. And Dad's *here* on the island, or he will be any moment. He's coming to this field.

"Stop!" I say. "That isn't your business! That isn't anyone's business."

"I mean, your dad put it on a public website, so it seems like it *is* anyone's business," Hannah says.

I reach for the phone, but Hannah holds it behind her back like a little kid playing keep-away.

"This is why you suddenly had to escape to Gray Island, huh?" she says. "Because you wanted to be somewhere no one knew your dad's a criminal." Her voice is casual, but her words are knives.

"He's not a criminal!" I say. "That isn't—"

"And it's why you were so determined to, like, be the camp MVP and bump Nia out of playing shortstop and con me into helping you plan this Slow Pitch Social so you could impress Coach Conway. So you could steal yourself a scholarship to go to school here?"

"Hannah, I'm sure that's not—" Nia cuts in, but Hannah ignores her.

"I actually thought we were becoming friends for a second there." Hannah shakes her head. "I should have realized your family only looks out for yourselves."

"That isn't true," I protest, reaching for the phone again but she spins away. "How did you find that statement?"

"There's this thing called Google," she says, but that's not a real answer. How did she know what to search for?

"Can you please just tell me—why did you search for my dad?" I beg, and Hannah rolls her eyes.

"My mom told me you're going through something because your dad got in trouble and then I went online and found the rest. She wanted me to give you the benefit of the doubt just like she's always doing with your mom, but

I'm done with that. My mom lets people take advantage of her. I don't."

I'm quiet as I let that sink in. Danielle told Hannah.

Who told Danielle? Mom? Aunt Mary? Has she known all along? She must not think Dad's wonderful anymore. No one here will, now.

"What's going on here?" Rose comes up behind us, and the other girls all back away. "Bea, Hannah? What's wrong?"

Hannah's face turns red. "Nothing. Everything's fine."

Rose raises her eyebrows. "Bea? You all right?"

I nod, and I guess Rose believes me. She pats my shoulder and tells everyone to head out to the outfield grass and circle up, so I stumble out there with the rest of the group.

Rose tells us she's proud of how hard we've worked and how much progress we've made. I'm trying to pay attention to what else she's saying, but Hannah's words keep echoing in my brain.

*Your family only looks out for yourselves.*

I really don't want that to be true.

Rose finishes talking, and people are clapping and standing.

"Bea?" Nia says, holding out a hand to pull me up. "You want to throw together?"

I don't want to throw the ball. Not now, when I can't think straight.

But I tell her sure and line up just like everybody else, because what other choice is there? Nia throws the ball to me, and I just hold it in my hand, terrified to let go. My brain spins through excuses and escape routes.

"Let's practice catching short hops!" I suggest.

That's when the ball bounces a few feet in front of you, and you have to adjust to make sure it bounces into your glove. If I'm throwing short hops, I can change up my motion and aim in front of Nia instead of at her.

"Um, okay," Nia says.

So we do short hops, then roll each other grounders, then lob the ball way up high to practice catching pop-ups.

"I'm going to throw normally now," she finally says. "Just to make sure my arm's warm."

She throws the ball right into my glove. And now I need to throw it back.

So I curl my arm and throw, as fast as I can, without leaving myself time to think. The ball flies way over Nia's head.

*Ack.*

I run after the ball and check the stands. People are trickling in. There are Nia's parents. There's Emery's dad, and there's Danielle. I don't know what Hannah's dad looks like, so I scan the crowd for a man I haven't seen before who's sitting by himself, but I don't spot anybody. My parents and Aunt Mary aren't here yet, but they will be, and I need to get myself together, *now*. I pick up the ball and jog it back to Nia, dropping it into her glove and then sprinting over to where I was standing before.

She tosses the ball to me, nice and easy. Because throwing a softball should be easy! I've been doing it successfully for years!

I curl my arm to throw it back, but the ball dives straight into the ground, not even five feet in front of me.

My heart is racing, and my brain spins. I'm sweating and shaky and I have to play in front of all these people, and I made so much progress but now it's gone. Wiped away. What am I supposed to do?

"Hey." Nia jogs over and picks up the ball. "Let's get some water real quick." She loops her arm through my elbow, and I try to zone out every other person here as she guides me over to the side of the field.

"I'm sorry. I don't know what's wrong with me," I mumble.

She gulps down a sip and then wipes a few drops off her chin. "You don't have to apologize."

I think of Mom, saying I shouldn't throw around apologies and give away my power. *Apologies are for expressing remorse when you regret something you've done.* That's what she's drilled into me.

But I definitely, definitely regret throwing the ball over Nia's head and then into the ground. And it feels like any power I had was gone way before I said the word "sorry."

"Do you want to talk about the stuff Hannah was saying or no?" Nia asks.

I shake my head.

"Okay. So listen, last winter, I suddenly forgot how to take a free throw. It was wild. I missed one and then when I went to take the next one, I thought 'Don't miss this one, too,' and I kept missing. Every single time. Not hitting the rim or the backboard or anything. *Really* missing."

Nia had the yips.

That lifts a tiny bit of my panic, knowing it happened to her, too, and she got through it. She's fine.

"What did you do?"

She takes another sip of water. "That person who was here last week—Dr. Alvarez? I had a few sessions with her. She helped me break apart the different stuff that was freaking me out so it wasn't, like, this massive cloud of worry. She helped me come up with an affirmation—something positive to break me out of the negative thought cycle. Like she was telling us."

But I don't know what she was telling us, because I took off and then zoned out. I put up gates around something that could have helped me. Why didn't I suck it up and listen?

"Now I count up to ten and then back down to one, too," Nia adds. "That's my ritual. I do it every time I'm at the foul line."

Like Rose had us do if we got off track during the meditating. That worked for me then. Maybe it'll work now.

"I'll try that," I say. "The counting."

We jog back out onto the field, and I close my eyes and count before I throw. The ball's only about a foot over Nia's head, so this time she can reach it, at least.

"Better!" she says.

I laugh, because the idea that I need praise for an off-target throw is ridiculous, and laughing relaxes me even more. My next throw goes straight into Nia's glove, and so does the one after that, and the one after that.

When warm-ups are done and we head off the field, I thank Nia for helping and spot my parents, walking toward the stands with Aunt Mary, who isn't limping at all anymore. Mom's wearing sunglasses, capri pants, and one of her favorite wrinkle-free shirts: short-sleeved and navy with an embroidered pattern around the hem. Dad's wearing a bright green polo that matches our Seagulls shirts because he's *Dad*, and he'll do anything in the world to support me, which means he texted earlier this week to ask what color my team was. Of *course* he found a shirt to match.

He sees me and pulls on his earlobe three times. *I. Love. You.*

I pull my earlobe three times back and will my too-fast heart to settle down.

"Those are your parents?" Nia says. "That's so nice they came. My mom will be happy to see your mom."

I smile and tell her yes, but I can't help wondering what she's really thinking. That Dad doesn't look like the kind of person who would steal? That Mom sure got a rough deal, losing her first husband and then marrying someone like that?

I want to convince Nia that Dad's a good person. I want to build a shield around my parents' seats so nobody can bother them. Pin up some signs like the ones in front of the dunes at the beach, telling everyone to keep away.

But they're over there and I'm over here, and there's nothing I can do except try not to fall apart.

"All right, Seagulls," Coach Conway says. "Almost game time. Let's go over the lineup."

I'm batting second and starting at short, just like when we scrimmaged. Coach Conway reminds us to be selective at the plate, to stay on our toes and be ready for the ball. "And most of all, have fun," he finishes.

But . . . *how*? I can't remember how going out on a field to play in front of people *ever* felt fun.

Thoughts come at me too fast to hold on to, like too many line drives pelted one after another, all just beyond my reach.

*I want to play. I'm scared to play. I'm so glad my parents are here. I wish they hadn't come.*

The Sandpipers get to be the home team this time, so they take their positions in the field. I grab my bat, jam my batting helmet down over my head, and make my way to the on-deck circle while Melanie walks up to the plate. The first pitch is low and outside. Melanie lays off, and everyone cheers.

"Good eye, Mel!" I shout, but I'm a beat too late. The pitcher's already winding up again.

This one's over the plate, and Melanie makes contact. She smacks a single down the first base line, which means she's on first and I'm up to bat. I don't think I remembered to take any practice swings, but it's too late now.

"Here we go, Bumble!" Dad cheers.

I tell myself this is good, coming up to bat before I take the field. I can get a quick hit. Calm my nerves. Help my team.

The first pitch is a little high—the kind Dad always reminds me to lay off. I hear his voice in my head telling me to let it go, but it looks too good and I'm too overeager. I swing and connect, and my heart sinks. It's a weak ground ball, right at Hannah.

*Mess up. Mess up*, I will her as I sprint down the first base line.

"Out! Out!" the umpire shouts. Someone on my team's bench groans, and all the Sandpipers cheer.

I hit into a double play.

Hannah threw to second, and their second baseman threw to first. That was literally the worst thing I could have done. Dad's holding his hands up, paused mid-clap, as if he was all ready to applaud for me before I swung at a pitch I should have laid off and served up two outs for my team.

I trudge back to the bench, where Coach Conway says, "It's okay, Bea. You'll get a hit next time."

*Will* I, though? Or am I going to start falling apart at the plate now, too?

Any confidence I got back when I was throwing with Nia is gone now. And I don't have time to get it back, because Emery strikes out and before I know it, we're taking the field.

Emery tosses a ball around the infield to warm our arms back up, and when the ball comes to me, I can't make myself throw it back to her. I roll it to Riley at third as if I'm giving her extra fielding practice, and then I want to smack myself in the face with my glove. If I don't have the guts to throw now, I have no shot on an actual play.

I promise myself I'll throw to first on my next turn, but right when Emery's about to give me the ball again, the umpire calls the Sandpipers' first batter up to the plate and Emery rolls it over to the bench.

I crouch into fielding position and glance out at Dad, who's leaning forward, shooting me a thumbs-up I don't deserve.

Tasha tries to slap bunt, but she knocks the ball right to Kaitlin. That's one easy out, and the second batter flies out to center field.

*Okay.* I imagine one of those big rainbow parachutes with all the handles that grown-ups used to hold on to at my gymnastics class when I was little. They'd raise the parachute up and down, and the kids would all run underneath as the silky fabric floated over our heads.

I'm not by myself, trying to keep the parachute in the air on my own. My teammates are holding the handles with me, raising the fabric off the ground. Even if I'm not at my best, we can do this together.

Kaitlin winds up for her next pitch, and I try Nia's counting trick. I'm up to seven when the ball pops off the hitter's bat, toward me.

I'm not on my toes. I'm back on my heels, not ready. Why am I not ready?

*Charge!* I tell myself, but my legs are heavy. I finally grab the ball and rush my throw. It's a little low, but it should beat the runner. Emery has to stretch, but she catches the ball, and—

"Safe!" the umpire shouts.

*What?*

He signals that Emery's foot came off the bag.

If I'd gotten to the ball faster—if my throw had been better—that would have been an out. It *should* have been an out.

Hannah comes up to bat and I pound my fist into my glove so hard my knuckles sting. She swings at the first pitch and misses. She doesn't swing at the next pitch, and it's a called strike down the middle.

Two outs, and there are two quick strikes on Hannah.

*Okay.* We can get out of this inning. Start fresh.

But then Kaitlin winds up and releases, and Hannah swings.

*Crack.*

The ball shoots off her bat, heading between me and Riley. I dive for it, hoping to make the catch so I won't have to throw, but the ball hits the ground before it reaches my glove. I pop up and glance at second base. I have no shot at getting the lead runner at second, but a good throw will get Hannah at first.

I start the counting trick to fight off my panic, but I don't have time to get up to ten and back to one. I need to throw *now*. Emery's waving her glove in the air, screaming for the ball.

I need to give Dad one thing to be happy about.

I need to earn that thumbs-up he gave me. I can't make things even worse.

I curl my arm back, throw as hard as I can, and . . . *no!*

There's a sickening thud. Someone shrieks. People on the sideline scatter.

My throw flew way past Emery, and *hard*. It hit someone on our bench. Somebody's on the *ground*.

It's *Nia*. My friend, who tried so hard to help me. Coach Rose and Coach Conway rush over with Nia's parents right behind them.

They help her sit up, and I can see now that she's holding her elbow as tears stream down her face. I put all my strength into that throw and hit her elbow—a *bone* with no flesh to protect it. What if her elbow's broken and she can't play basketball because of me?

On the field, the umpire says it's a dead ball. He has the two runners take one more base each, stopping on second and third, and then calls a time-out. Everyone clusters together in the middle of the diamond, but I can't go stand with the rest of my teammates. I can't face Nia. I don't have any idea *what* to do. So I run.

## CHAPTER 24

I run past school buildings, over grassy hills, and between dorms. Finally, I reach a small, wooded area at the edge of campus with a fence just past the trees. I can't go any farther, so I stop in front of the tallest tree with the thickest trunk. I sit on the ground, curl my body into a ball, and let myself cry.

I cry gulping, wailing, body-emptying sobs. My tears stream down my face and soak my dirt-stained shirt.

"Everything's out of control," I say out loud to the trunk of the tree once I'm finally done crying. "I'm out of control. I've lost control!"

It's what I've been afraid of this whole time: losing control of my ability to throw the ball, losing control of my mind, losing control of what everyone else thinks. All of that has happened, and it feels absolutely, excruciatingly terrible.

But also: I'm still here. My heart is still beating, my feet are still resting on solid ground, my lungs are still breathing in air.

Mom's always insisted that I get to control *me*, no matter what happens, but . . . maybe that's wrong. Maybe sometimes feelings are too big and worries are too loud and mistakes are too humiliating, and you can't tame them into something manageable.

Maybe it *isn't* such a shameful thing to lose control sometimes because the only alternative is putting up a whole lot of gates and closing yourself off.

I hear Dad's voice calling my name, and then Mom's voice, too. I stand up and see them—about as far away as the distance from home plate to the outfield. They're running toward me, Dad in his Seagulls-green shirt and Mom with her practical, no-wrinkle top and pressed-together lips.

So many emotions clobber me, and for once I don't try to squash the horrible ones. I let them all in, and more tears come.

Dad gets to me first and hugs me long and tight. "There you are. Thank goodness. Are you okay?"

I take an enormous psych-up breath, and then I tell him, "No. I'm not okay."

Mom's forehead crinkles when she hears that. She hugs me, too, and reaches out to wipe the tears from my cheeks, but I step back instead of letting her.

"You're going to be all right, Bea," she tells me. "The girl who got hit with the ball is fine. She's shaken up, but the trainer thinks it's a bruise, that's all. So many things are so hard right now, honey, but you're okay. *We're* okay."

Her eyes are begging me to agree. It would be so easy to say, "Yes, you're right. I'm okay. We're the better-than-a-dream team, so of course we're okay."

But I *am* strong and brave, like Mom is always saying. Or I want to be, anyway. So I don't say any of that.

"No," I say instead. "I'm not okay." I look over at Dad. "And I'm not the best kid in the world. I didn't hang the moon. I'm a kid who's trying my hardest. And sometimes I'm doing a good job and sometimes I'm not. And . . . I don't think you're okay, either. Neither of you are. Can we just—can we just be not okay together? Please?"

Mom presses her lips together even more tightly, and Dad puts his head in his hands.

His shoulders are shaking. He's crying, and it pierces my heart to watch him cry.

"Henry," Mom says, her tone stern.

I want to reassure him. I want to bring him joy and make sure nobody hurts his feelings or writes a mean comment about him on Instagram.

But I can't.

I think what Aunt Mary said last night is true. It isn't my job to make my parents happy because it *can't* be. There are too many variables outside my control, and if I keep trying, I'll drop too many other balls. I'll drop all the ones that bring *me* joy.

"*Henry*," Mom says again, and now her voice is a plea instead of a warning.

Dad wipes his cheeks with the sleeve of his bright green shirt. He takes in an enormous psych-up breath, and then he squeezes my hand. "You're right, Bea. I'm not okay either. I'm so sorry for what I've put you through. I'm so ashamed."

He starts crying again, and he isn't covering his face this time. Mom closes her eyes and breathes in and out, doing her "calm and in control" self-regulating, probably, and then she starts pacing. I have the urge to grab her shoulders so she has to stand still—to scream at her to stop self-regulating and be *real*.

Because, yes, it's scary to watch Dad's face twist up and turn red as tears fall down his clean-shaven cheeks.

But it was even scarier to feel the way I did when I read Mom's essay—like there are these huge important things I just don't know, and I have no clue what other secrets might pop up next.

"I've started going to therapy again," Dad says in a shaky voice. "It's helping me. To work through how I let things get so bad and what to do next—in terms of my job but also just in terms of . . . forgiving myself in some way. Maybe all three of us could go to a session together. Or you could go on your own, Bea. Or both."

That sounds scary, too, honestly, but the kind of scary that could help me if I'm brave enough to try. Like Coach Rose's guided meditations, and Dr. Alvarez's strategies, and Aunt Mary's art. "I think that would be good. Yeah. And I'm sorry I kept asking and asking if I could go to the sleepaway camp even though it was so expensive. I didn't mean to make you even more stressed about money."

Mom stops pacing. Dad's eyes go wide and he grips my hand tighter. "Oh, Bea, no. You didn't do anything wrong. I'm responsible for what happened. Not you. Not anyone else. Only me, and I am so, so sorry."

Part of me wants to say that other people are a little bit at fault, too—the clients who didn't pay their bills on time, and Gran for making him feel so much pressure, and the big firm that acquired his old firm and didn't want him.

But Dad made the choice to open his own practice even though it was risky, and Dad didn't follow the rules.

"Are you depressed?" I ask him.

He glances at Mom, who's shifting her weight from one foot to the other, as if her legs want to go back to pacing but she isn't letting her feet leave the ground.

"Maybe," Dad says. "I've . . . I've been depressed in the past. This isn't quite the same, the way things are now. But my therapist thinks I might be. I'm going to see a psychiatrist to talk about medication. But I'll . . ." He trails off.

*But I'll be okay.*

I'm sure that's what he was going to say, but he stopped himself. Because he's letting himself be not-okay with me, like I asked him to, not speeding ahead of where we are.

"I know," I say quietly. "That you were depressed before." I turn to Mom. "And I know what happened with Evan."

Mom stares at me. "You *what*?"

"I read your essay. The one about Evan and Dad and Aunt Mary. Someone said something about what happened to Evan, and I found it online. So I know now. What Evan was sick with, and that he grew up here."

She opens her mouth, closes it, and opens it again.

"That essay," she finally says. "Oh, Bea. Sweetheart."

I wait for her to string enough words together to

complete an actual sentence, but she doesn't say anything else.

"Why didn't you tell me the truth?" I ask, and my voice comes out angry.

She shakes her head. "This isn't the place," she says. "Here, back on the island . . . all those people back at the field . . ."

Dad reaches for her hand with the hand that isn't holding mine. I tell myself I should reach for her other hand so the three of us are linked together in a triangle. Our team. But I don't want to hold Mom's hand if she won't be real with me. She only holds Dad's for a second, anyway, and then she pulls away and takes out her phone.

"I'm going to text Aunt Mary to meet us back at the car. Maybe we can get on a ferry later today. Get back home where we can think straight. We'll talk about everything when we're home."

She's trying to take control.

She's trying to yank us out of this hard moment and away from this whole island, but I'm not going to let her.

"No," I say. "I don't want to leave."

"Bea. You ran away from that field. You were beside yourself when we found you. This is too much. All that pressure. All these hard, sad things. It's. Too. Much." Her voice gets louder and louder, and she sounds so absolutely certain. But that doesn't mean she's right.

"No!" I shout. "You were wrong to lie to me about Evan and you're wrong now."

She gasps. "Bea Bartlett," she scolds, but I'm not done.

"If it's too much for *you* to talk about Evan while we're here on Gray Island, then fine. I'll ask you again when we're back in New Jersey. But I'm not leaving."

"What do you want to do, Bea?" Dad asks.

I close my eyes and picture myself walking off the field at the championship game back in New Jersey. I picture myself losing control of that throw and hitting Nia.

It hurts—so much—to hold those two images in my brain. My muscles tense and my stomach squeezes and my body is begging me to push those memories away. But I don't.

I try to breathe in love for myself, even though I'm still not really sure what that means. I tell myself what Aunt Mary would say: that I'm a good kid. That I'm going through a hard time, but I'm doing my best.

I know in my gut that doing my best means going back to that field.

"I want to go back to the game," I tell my parents.

Mom takes in a sharp breath. "Bea. Honey. I don't think—"

"It's what I need to do," I insist.

A slow smile spreads across Dad's face, which is still blotchy from crying. "Oh, Bea. You are . . ."

He pauses, and I will him *not* to tell me I'm the best kid in the world.

"You are one strong, brave person," he finishes.

Mom straightens her posture and nods. She closes her eyes, breathes in and out, and in a whisper, she tells me, "Go get 'em, Bumble."

I hug them both, and then I run as fast as I can, back to the field.

CHAPTER

25

The Seagulls are in the field when I get back to the game. Melanie's at shortstop, where she never, ever plays, and Izzy's at second base instead of out in right field.

But the scoreboard tells me the game's tied 2–2 in the bottom of the sixth. The Seagulls have hung in there without me.

Nia's sitting on the bench with ice wrapped around her elbow. I rush over to see how she's doing and apologize, but before I get there, Kaitlin strikes out the last batter of the inning and the whole team jogs off the field.

"Bea! You're back!" Emery says.

"She can play shortstop for the last inning, right?" Melanie asks Coach Conway. "How strict are we being about substitution rules? Because I'd *really* like to go back to second."

Coach Conway looks right at me, eyebrows raised. I've disappointed him, and I can't change that. But I *can* decide what I do next.

"I'd love to play short for the last inning if it's allowed. But first, I'm so sorry, Nia. Are you okay?"

Nia nods. "I know you didn't do it on purpose. It hurts, but it's better now. I'll be all right."

I give her a hug, and then I face everyone else. "I'm really sorry I took off. I came here trying to get away from some pretty hard things at home. Family stuff, like what Hannah found out about, and throwing error stuff, too. I can't guarantee I won't throw the ball away again. I understand if you want me to just watch and cheer you on after I bailed like that, but I'll play if you want me to play. I'll do the best I can."

Nobody says anything at first. I look from one person to another—Nia, Melanie, Emery, Izzy, Coach Conway. And behind him, Coach Rose.

"That low throw in the first inning was totally catchable," Emery says. "I shouldn't have let it pull me off the base. I'll make the play next time even if you throw off-line—promise. You're a Seagull, and we need you."

"And I *really* don't want to play second base." Izzy shudders. "I'm still traumatized by that line drive Hannah hit directly at my head."

"You caught it, though!" Emery reminds her.

Izzy shakes her head. "I have *no* idea how. Anyway. Bea's the main reason I can sort of throw and hit now." She looks at Coach Conway. "No offense. So I definitely want her to play."

"Me too," Nia says.

"Same here."

"Me too."

Everyone's nodding and agreeing, and my heart swells, but then I glance out toward the stands, where my parents are walking back to their seats. I picture the word "nerves" at the top of Dr. Alvarez's sports anxiety cycle, leading into all the other bad stuff.

"I'm really nervous," I admit. "I might mess up again."

"What's the absolute worst-case scenario, though?" Nia holds up her elbow with the ice pack wrapped around it. "The worst has probably happened."

I wince and apologize again, but Nia grins and eventually I crack a smile, too.

"Seems like we've got consensus," Coach Conway says, patting me on the back. "Bea goes back in at short. Now, let's finish strong here. Let's win this thing. *Caw, caw, caw!*"

He makes a little beak with one hand as he does our chant, which makes everyone laugh. We gather around for a team cheer, and then we all *caw-caw* as Emery goes up to bat to lead off the inning.

My spot in the batting order just came up last inning when I was gone, so there's almost no chance I'm going to get a turn to hit. Emery gets a single, but then our next two batters get out. Riley doubles to drive Emery in, so by the time we're back in the field, we're up, 3–2.

It's almost exactly the same situation we were in at the semifinals, back at home. My team's up one run. If we keep our opponents from scoring, we win.

While Kaitlin takes warm-up pitches, Emery rolls the ball to Melanie at second, and then to me. I throw it back, soft but on target, and Emery shoots me a thumbs-up. I think of that multicolored parachute from little-kid gymnastics again—everyone holding a handle, working together to keep the fabric in the air.

I'm not alone out here. I only have to hold one handle. And even if I let my handle go, even if I mess up again, I'll survive.

The ump calls for the other team's first batter, and I *want* to want the ball, but I'm not sure I actually do.

"No outs, Seagulls! Play's to first," I call.

"Yeah, Seagulls!" Emery yells from first base. "We've got this!"

The first batter grounds out to Melanie at second, so there's one down right away.

The second batter walks, which means the tying run's on base.

Hannah steps up to the plate. She taps the end of her bat against the ground before pulling it over her back shoulder, and anger flashes in my gut as I watch her settle into her stance.

I'm mad at myself for what she heard me say outside the Creamery, but I'm even madder at her for what she did before the game. That anger dims my nerves just a little.

*I want to make the play*, I tell myself, and I'm pretty sure I do.

Hannah swings and rockets the first pitch down the third base line, just foul. Riley, who's playing third, looks at me with her eyes wide and mouths, "Phew."

That would have been an extra base hit if it had stayed fair.

The next pitch is a wild pitch that Paige can't block. It bounces all the way to the backstop behind home plate, and the runner at first advances to second, giving Hannah a good chance to drive in a run and tie the game.

"That's all right, Kaitlin!" I say. "You've got this."

She winds up, and the next pitch is soft and down the middle. A perfect pitch to hit. Hannah swings so hard she nearly loses her grip on the bat, and the ball soars sky-high toward shallow center field.

She popped it up.

Our center fielder, Jasmine, plants herself in the right spot and makes the easy catch.

Any hit probably would have scored a run. But Hannah tried to hit a home run and got out. She throws her bat into the ground, hard, and throws her helmet, too.

"Hey now, careful there!" the umpire says. He gives her a warning, and she storms off toward the end of her team's bench. She wasn't close to anybody else, but umpires don't mess around when you throw a bat. She's lucky she didn't get tossed out of the game.

"Here we go, Seagulls!" Nia calls from the bench. "One more out!"

I'm calmer as the next batter comes to the plate. I definitely want the ball now.

Kaitlin's pitch is hard and low. The batter swings, connects . . . and pops up foul, down the first base line. Emery's got a shot at catching it if she can get there fast enough, but it's going to be tough. She sprints past our bench and dives, stretching out horizontal. She catches the ball in the tip of her glove and hits the grass hard.

That kind of glove-to-ground contact usually knocks the ball free, but Emery hangs on. She lifts her glove in the air to show that she still has the ball, and our team erupts in cheers.

"Out!" the umpire shouts, and Emery's dad screams, "That's my kid! Did you see that? That's my girl!"

I wonder if Hannah's dad is here, too. I'm not sure if it would be worse if he showed up to see her lose or if he didn't come at all.

All my teammates jump in the air, cheering and shouting. We run over to Emery and pile on. Emery's the hero today. She deserves all the praise and congratulations everyone's giving her. I didn't do a single thing to help my team win. We won in spite of me, not because of me, and that stings.

We line up to tell the Sandpipers good game, and Coach Rose pulls me aside before I go back to join my teammates.

"That took a lot of guts, coming back out onto the field," she says. "I'm proud of you, Bea."

She says it like she really means it, and I let her words sink in.

I didn't get any hits. I didn't make any good throws. But getting back out there on the field even though I was terrified and embarrassed—I think maybe that was gutsier than any play I've ever made. I think maybe I'm proud, too.

## CHAPTER 26

When we get back to Aunt Mary's, I'm so exhausted that I can barely keep my eyes open. I tell everyone I'm going to lie down for a few minutes and wake up to find two hours have passed.

Dad's by himself in the kitchen when I go downstairs.

"Hey, she's awake!" he greets me, motioning to the deck, where Mom and Aunt Mary are deep in conversation. "Was this all part of your master plan? Pretending to take a nap so Mom and Aunt Mary would have a good long chat?"

I laugh. "Something like that?"

After I eat a sandwich, we decide to go for a beach walk to give them more time just the two of them. On the way out the door, he pulls his softball glove out of his bag. "What do you think?" he asks, holding it up.

I hesitate for a second, but then I nod.

"Sure, bring it. I'll go grab mine."

We head down the path to the beach, past the dunes where I lost the picture of Allison and past a couple of kids not much younger than I am, throwing a football back and forth.

As we walk, Dad tells me about the condos he and Mom looked at back at home. They're on the other side of Butler, way farther out from the center of town. Still in the same school district, but barely. The units are small but new and pretty with big windows and lots of light. We wouldn't have our own yard anymore, though. There wouldn't be a place right out back for Mom to have a vegetable garden and Dad and me to throw.

"It would be temporary," he says. "Mom and I are thinking we'd rent one for a year. Get you through eighth grade at Butler Middle, and then decide what makes sense next."

"Like, maybe not living in Butler?" I ask, and he sighs.

"The truth is, we aren't sure, Bumble. There are a lot of unknowns right now. A lot of hard choices we'll need to make."

I bend down to pick up an ice cream sandwich wrapper that's half buried in the sand and put it in my pocket so I can throw it away when we see a trash can.

"Would it be easier for you to go somewhere different now?" I ask. "Without the Bartlett Benches in the middle of town and all these people who know every detail about your life?"

He shades his eyes from the sun and looks out at the water for a few seconds before he answers. "In a lot of ways, yes," he says. "But I don't want to run away in shame. I won't suddenly uproot you from your school and all your friends. I want us to make the next choice as a family."

I watch a seagull scuttle across the shoreline and pick something up in its beak.

"I think I kind of ran away. By coming here, I mean," I say. "I had this whole fantasy that we could move here for good. Start over and never go back. It's silly."

"Trust me, I get it." He stops walking, so I do, too. He sets down his glove and hugs me, long and tight. "I've let you down," he says into my ear. "I've let a lot of people down, myself included, but I want to make things right, as much as I can. I want you to be proud of me again. I want to be proud of myself again."

When he pulls out of the hug, there's a tear rolling down his cheek.

I want so much to tell him that he hasn't let me down and I'm still proud of him. But the truth is, I *haven't* felt proud of him lately. He *did* let me down.

I sync my breath to the swish of the little waves—in and

out, in and out—and I look out at the water that seems to go on forever.

The ocean gives me a different kind of perspective check than Allison's photo did. I know other places exist way out past all this water, but I can't see them from here. I know so many other people have stood on this sand looking out at the horizon as cold, salty water rushes over their feet. They've made mistakes, they've lost people they love, they've found joy so big it feels better than a dream. And all that time, the ocean's been here, moving and changing, but constant, too.

I used to think that if I took advantage of every opportunity and accomplished impressive things, then that would make it worth it somehow, that Allison and Evan are gone and I'm here. As if I could earn my spot as a human who exists in this universe.

But I can't make up for them being gone. I can't take away the pain my parents have been through. I'm not obligated to be a great softball player or a perfect daughter, because I have to make the most of the life I'm lucky to have.

But I *want* to be a good player and a good daughter. I want to be a good person and try my best and give myself compassion when I come up short. I want to give other people compassion when *they* come up short, too.

"I love you, Dad," I tell him, because that's the truth, no matter what.

"I love you too, Bumble," he replies. "More than I know how to say."

I look down at his glove sitting on the sand. Before this summer, we'd never gone more than a few days without having a catch, and now it's been weeks.

"You up for throwing the ball?" I ask him, and he smiles. "Always."

We put our gloves on our hands, and Dad backs up and tosses me the ball. I breathe in and out with the rhythm of the ocean, tell those yips I won't let them steal what I love, and throw the ball back, right into his glove.

A little while later, as we're walking back toward the house, Jessi calls.

"Is it okay if I meet you back at Aunt Mary's?" I ask Dad. "I really need to talk to Jessi."

He says that's fine and to tell her hi, and while he keeps walking, I sit in the sand near the dunes and pick up.

"Hey," I say, drawing circles in the sand with one finger and searching my brain for the right words to fix everything between Jessi and me.

"So I'm still upset," she says back. "And you probably

are, too. But we should put that on hold for, like, a minute and talk about how upset *Xander* is because you told him not to come to some slow pitch something or other? And you pulled away when he tried to hold your hand?"

My finger stops mid-circle. "I . . . wait. What?"

"He's texted me so many times to ask whether I've heard from you and if I think he made you uncomfortable and whether you hate him because you told him he'd ruin some event you planned? Bea. What happened when Xander tried to hold your hand?"

"He didn't try to hold my hand for real," I tell her. "It was a pity hand hold."

"I don't think he would text me multiple times about a pity hand hold," she points out, and I can't help it: My heart speeds up and my skin goes warm.

"I was really thrown off when he suddenly showed up."

"Which is why I tried to warn you," she says, and I wince.

"I'm sorry I didn't let you. And I'm really, really sorry I didn't tell you about the camp, Jess. I'm really sorry I can't room with you."

She sighs. "I know. I'm sorry I kept saying the wrong thing before you left. I want to be there for you. I couldn't figure out how."

"I know."

We're both quiet for a little while. Down at the edge of the water, a girl in a yellow bathing suit grabs another girl's hand and yells, "One, two, three, go!" and they run into the ocean together, squealing and splashing.

"I'm getting home Monday," I say. "We'll have a couple weeks to hang out, right? Before the sleepaway camp starts. I'm in for the next Sugihara pastabilities night, or I'll keep you company babysitting the twins. Anything. I'll even watch one of those scary movies you like so much."

"There's a new one I want to see but I'm nervous to watch by myself," she says.

"Done. And . . . we'll talk for real," I tell her, because we have to, even if it's sad and weird at first. I can't close myself off to Jessi.

"Okay. Good," she says. "But for now, throw Xander a bone and text him, will you?"

I laugh. "I will. Promise."

We end the call, and I burrow my toes into the sand. I take a psych-up breath, find Xander's number in my contacts, and type.

*Hey. I was really surprised when I saw you the other day and I didn't react well. I'm sorry I told you not to come to the Slow Pitch Social. If you want to come, you should.*

Xander replies almost immediately. *Do you want me to come?*

Then he sends another message: *My dad's going fishing tomorrow, just so you know. He won't be around.*

I'm about to gnaw straight through the inside of my cheek, but I type, *Yes. I want you to come.* And then I press Send before I can chicken out.

*In that case, I'll be there*, he says.

And even though I tell myself things are way too complicated to get giddy over Xander, I can't stop smiling as I walk back to the house.

·

After dinner, we take out some old photo albums Aunt Mary found in the attic.

One of them has a bunch of old school portraits—each marked with the year and what grade Mom and Aunt Mary were in. While Mom and Dad are busy looking at an album full of baby pictures, I find the picture of Mom in eighth grade.

Thirteen-year-old Mom didn't have poufy bangs like Allison. Her hair was so long it kept going past the bottom of the photo, and she smiled with her mouth closed. Grown-up-Mom would tell eighth-grade Mom to smile for real and be herself, because a person is beautiful when she's comfortable in her own skin. But eighth-grade Mom wasn't there yet. Maybe some of the time, grown-up Mom isn't, either.

I take out my phone to snap a picture of the photo, and Aunt Mary notices.

"Do you want to keep it?" she asks, and I nod.

I don't know quite how to explain *why* I want it, but Aunt Mary doesn't ask for an explanation. She just slides it out of the plastic and hands it to me.

"Your mom mentioned you might not have a ton going on later this summer, since you aren't going to that sleep-away camp with your friends. You always have an open invitation to come back here if you want to. If you aren't tired of me after two weeks, that is." She grins. "And if you aren't sick of pasta."

"I'm definitely not tired of you, and I told you, I really like pasta," I tell her. "I still need to introduce you to this thing my friend's family does, pastabilities night. It's a whole experience."

She laughs. "That sounds pretty spectacular." Then she winks. "You could even join me for an art class, if you're up for it. Think about it."

"Thank you," I say. "For letting me stay with you and

inviting me back, and . . . for so many things. I don't even know where to start. The art and the sunsets and all the rides to and from camp. Everything."

"It's been my pleasure." She gives me a hug and whispers, "And thank you for bringing your mom back. Not that it was your responsibility to help us reconcile. But you opened your heart to me and to Gray Island, and that helped your mom open her heart, too."

## CHAPTER 27

In the morning, I wake up to the sound of footsteps padding down the hallway. Mom's footsteps—lighter and quicker than Dad's or Aunt Mary's.

I throw a sweatshirt on over my pajamas and follow her downstairs, where she's putting on a pot of coffee. "Hey," she says. "You're up early."

I pour myself a glass of water and sit down at the table. "You, too."

"Do you remember when you found out about Allison's car accident?" she asks, sitting down next to me. "How scared you were?"

Her question catches me completely off guard, but I do remember.

It was second grade. I already knew Allison had died, and I think I'd known in a hazy sort of way that there'd been a car accident. But that year, her family planned a 5K run in Butler to raise money for an organization that gives presentations about safe driving, and I got sort of obsessed with what had happened.

I wanted to know everything—where the accident had been, what kind of car she'd been driving, what had happened to the truck driver who'd hit her, and most of all, how I could be sure that Mom and Dad would never get into an accident. For weeks, I hated it when either of my parents got in a car without me. I panicked that they wouldn't be safe if they drove when there was rain or snow.

"That's why I thought it would be better to be vague about Evan," Mom says, tracing a fingertip along the edge of the table. "I thought that would be less scary, to say he was sick and leave out the details. I'm not trying to make excuses for keeping secrets from you. But . . . I didn't know how to explain what had happened to a kid."

The coffee pot gurgles, filling the room with its nutty smell. Mom looks exhausted. Her face is pale, and I can see the graying roots of her hair, where the reddish-brown highlights have grown out.

"It isn't just that you didn't tell me about Evan, though," I say. "The whole time I've been here, I kept finding out all these things I didn't know about you. Little stuff about things you used to like. Plus the big stuff about Evan. It just felt like . . . do I even know you at all?"

Mom's mouth drops open. "Oh, Bea. Of course you know me."

She squeezes my hand. Her fingers are soft and a little chilly, just like always, and she smells like the moisturizer she puts on her face every night.

"Well, but I barely knew Aunt Mary before this summer. I'd barely spent any time on Gray Island at all, because *you* wanted to keep your past all gated off." The words come out sounding like an accusation and I wince, but Mom nods slowly.

Across the room, the coffee maker beeps. Dad always teases Mom about how she's so desperate for caffeine in the morning that she can never wait for the pot to finish brewing before she pours her first cup. She doesn't get up from the table now, though, and she doesn't wipe away the tears that glide down her cheeks.

"You're right," she says. "It's a hard thing for me, being back here. And there's a lot that's . . . not easy for me to talk about. But I'll work on that, okay? I'm sorry you didn't get to know Aunt Mary before this summer. That's on me."

And I think it means more when Mom apologizes than when anyone else does. I know she really means her sorrys.

Eventually, she stands to pour her coffee and I help myself to yogurt and granola.

"I need to tell you something," I say as we sit back down to eat. "I planned something big for today. I was hoping it was going to be this really special surprise for you and Dad. But now I'm not sure it's actually something you'll like. I don't want you to have to pretend to be happy about it if you aren't."

I explain about the Slow Pitch Social, and she sets down her coffee mug without even taking a sip. "Wait. You planned an entire Slow Pitch Social in two weeks?"

"One week, really. I only got the idea last weekend. I had a lot of help, though. And it'll be pretty low-key."

"Still," she says. "Wow."

"Good wow or bad wow?" I ask. "Does it sound like too much?"

Mom takes a long sip of coffee. "Good wow. And . . . it might be a lot. But I wouldn't miss it for the world."

"You sure?" I ask, and she nods and reaches out to hold both my hands in hers.

"If you could go back on that softball field yesterday, then I can do this."

It isn't a great afternoon for the Slow Pitch Social. It's chilly and gray with a chance of rain. People are scrambling to find trash bags and hand sanitizer, and we're short one vendor table, so someone has to rush inside to find another.

But there's a good turnout, and people seem to be having fun mingling before things start. I watch Mom hug Coach Conway and stop to talk to Meg from the bakery. She's wearing her glued-on smile and she never once stands still, but she's okay. Or maybe she's not all the way okay, actually, but *that's* okay.

"Hey," somebody says.

I turn around and there's Hannah.

"I wanted to say I'm sorry," she says, fidgeting with the neck of her T-shirt. "That was really awful, what I did yesterday. I shouldn't have read that to everyone. It was so mean."

I nod. "I shouldn't have said that thing about getting a scholarship, either. I don't have one, just so you know. I couldn't take one even if I did."

She shrugs. "Not like that means I have any shot at getting one after yesterday. Coach Conway thinks I'm a terrible sport. Definitely not Gray Island Academy material."

I shrug, too. "Maybe things will turn around for the

Creamery so you won't need the Academy. Or maybe you'll win Coach Conway over."

She raises her eyebrows. "I don't know. I hope so."

"I hope so, too," I say.

And I really do. I hate what she did, and I don't know if we'll ever be real friends now. But deep down, I think she's a good person who's having a hard time and trying her best, just like me. And I need to remember all the things I have that she doesn't. My parents are together. Dad's business fell apart and we're going to have to move, but my parents can still afford a condo in our nice town and Gran could probably loan them money. I hate the idea that Dad's some privileged jerk, but he *is* privileged in a lot of ways, and so am I.

More kids and families start to show up. Emery and Izzy arrive, and Nia, who has her softball bag over her shoulder, which hopefully means her elbow's better enough for her to play.

And Xander. He's wearing a royal blue T-shirt and a red Butler Baseball hat, and the shy, sweet smile on his face makes my stomach somersault. He waves, and I walk over.

"You're here," I say.

"I'm here."

My heart is beating so loud that I can't think straight, but I manage to tell him, "I'm glad."

"Yeah? And . . . you're not really moving here to Gray Island, right?"

I shake my head. "There was a tiny moment when I thought maybe. But no. We're moving somewhere else in Butler I think."

"Then *I'm* glad."

He's standing so close to me, and his warm brown eyes are looking right into mine. I want to count those green and copper glints. Memorize every single one.

"Even though everything's all complicated, because of my dad, and your dad?" I ask.

Before he can answer, Coach Conway calls for everybody's attention to welcome us. He starts talking about the event's history and how much it means to have everybody here now.

Xander leans down and whispers into my ear, "Even though all of that. Yeah."

His breath on my skin sends that static electricity buzz down to my toes, and when I turn my head up toward him and our eyes catch, everything on this field except him and me goes blurry. He slides his fingers through mine and squeezes once before letting go.

Coach Conway explains the logistics. We'll be having an all-ages, all-gender, all-skill-level game, and everyone who wants to play will line up on the field to get divided into teams.

"But first, I'd like to ask our two co-organizers, Bea Bartlett and Hannah Rogers, to come on out so we can show them some appreciation for their hard work."

Xander gives me a little nudge, so I jog out to the middle of the field to meet Hannah. Everyone is clapping, and so much adrenaline courses through my body—the good kind and the freaking-out kind all mingled together.

I pull my earlobe three times to tell my parents I love them, and I wave to Rose, who's in the back of the crowd, and Aunt Mary, who's standing with Linda.

I have no clue what's going to happen when we take the field to play this game. I might be fine. I might self-destruct. And I don't know what's going to happen between Xander and me or when our house will sell or where we'll live after next year. This is nothing like those directed drawings where I'm sure that as long as I follow the steps, I'll end up with something pretty.

But I have my glove in my hand, and I'm about to play the game I love, surrounded by all these people I care about.

I'm going to make throwing errors. If not today during this pickup game, then soon. And I'm going to make mistakes off the field, too. I'll come up short in all sorts of ways, because everybody does.

But I'm going to try to brush off my mistakes when they're the kind of mistakes you can brush off and apologize and make things right when they're not.

I'm going to want the ball to come to me when this game begins.

I'm ready to play.

# ACKNOWLEDGMENTS

Bea's story came to me with an urgency and sense of excitement I'd never experienced before, and working on this book has sustained me and challenged me in all the best ways throughout much of 2020 and 2021. I'm so grateful to everyone who has nurtured this novel and helped me find pockets of writing time along the way.

Thank you to Myles and Clint for title brainstorming, and thank you to Mike for sharing your legal expertise and being my problem-solving partner. Thank you to Jenn Barnes, Cindy Baldwin, and Laura Sibson for your insightful and encouraging feedback as well as your support and friendship. Thank you to Mia Cohen, my softball expert, for your valuable input, and thank you to Coach Sue Sweeney, Coach Chuck Coe, Coach Drew Burns, and my favorite softball teammate Marissa Litwin Zalk for making my own softball-playing days so fun and memorable.

Cordelia Jensen and Melissa Sarno, trusted readers and treasured friends, thank you for your astute, generous, and quick notes that tightened and enriched this novel (and added in a few LOLs, I hope, Cordelia).

Sara Crowe, thank you for your enthusiasm and advocacy, always. Maggie Lehrman, thank you for loving this story and guiding it where I always wanted it to go by asking smart, compassionate questions and pinpointing exactly where I could dig deeper. I'm grateful to the whole team at Abrams, including Andrew Smith, Jody Mosley, Emily Daluga, Brooke Shearouse, Jenny Choy, Kim Lauber, Megan Carlson, Jenn Jimenez, and Deena Fleming. Thanks, also, to Mike Burdick for the terrific cover illustration!

This book simply would not exist without my mom, Elizabeth Morrison, the world's greatest Grammy, who took such loving care of Cora and Sam while I wrote and revised. Thank you. We love you and are endlessly appreciative of all you do.

And Mike, Cora, and Sam: Even on the toughest, most exhausting days, you are my better-than-a-dream team. Thank you for bringing me joy, making me laugh, and helping me see wonder, beauty, and stories in places I wouldn't have thought to look.

## ABOUT THE AUTHOR

Laurie Morrison taught middle school for ten years before writing *Every Shiny Thing*, her middle-grade debut, with coauthor Cordelia Jensen. She is also the author of *Up for Air* and *Saint Ivy*. She received her MFA in writing for children and young adults from the Vermont College of Fine Arts. She lives in Philadelphia, Pennsylvania.